Ken was engaged to Lucille Duparc!

Caroline told herself she would have expected Kennedy Marshall to show more taste and judgment, but that seemed a poor reason for the shock and despair she was experiencing. She knew now, of course, that he was a man of generosity and sensitivity. How could such a man be content with a grasping and temperamental prima donna like Lucille?

I should hate him to be unhappy, she thought. *He's been so good to me in many ways. I like him and...*

Then she stared at her reflection in the mirror and faced the truth about herself.

"Don't be a fool," she said aloud. "You love him." And she buried her head in her hands.

Books by Mary Burchell

HARLEQUIN ROMANCE

HARLEQUIN PRESENTS

These books may be available at your local bookseller.

Don't miss any of our special offers. Write to us at the following address for information on our newest releases.

Harlequin Reader Service
P.O. Box 52040, Phoenix, AZ 85072-2040
Canadian address: P.O. Box 2800, Postal Station A,
5170 Yonge St., Willowdale, Ont. M2N 6J3

On Wings of Song

Mary Burchell

Harlequin Books

TORONTO • NEW YORK • LONDON
AMSTERDAM • PARIS • SYDNEY • HAMBURG
STOCKHOLM • ATHENS • TOKYO • MILAN

Original hardcover edition published in 1985
by Mills & Boon Limited

ISBN 0-373-02707-9

Harlequin Romance first edition August 1985

CHAPTER ONE

IF she had not lost her footing, running to escape the sudden downpour of rain, Caroline would never have noticed the ring. It was lying there on the grass verge beside the path and, as she struggled to her knees, wet and a good deal shaken by her fall, she realised that the something sparkling there was not just another raindrop. It was a diamond. A large diamond at that, most beautifully set in a ring of undoubted distinction.

'It can't be real!' was her first thought as she reached for it. But she knew it was. If it had been just any old diamond ring she might have been mistaken. But not with this one. The light which struck back from the stone proclaimed its proud identity, and instinctively she slipped the ring on to her finger instead of thrusting it into her handbag.

Then she scrambled to her feet, ignoring the pain in her wrenched ankle, and looked around the deserted paths of St James's Park. In the distance the last of the homegoing crowds were running into Piccadilly and the shelter of buses or Underground. Even if she could have caught up with them, which was doubtful, a general query of 'Has anyone lost a diamond ring?' would almost certainly result in an embarrassing number of claimants, from which she could not possibly identify the right one.

She would go to the police in the morning, she

told herself, or look for some newspaper announcement in the 'Lost and Found' column. At the moment all she wanted was to get home and into dry clothes. So she made for her bus, and was thankful to sink into the one unoccupied seat.

By the time she put her key into the lock of the front door she was feeling less sick and shaken, but a wave of irritation swept over her as Aunt Hilda called out predictably, 'Is that you, Caroline?'

Not for the first time she resisted the temptation to ask crossly who else it could be, and went into the front room, where her aunt was sitting idly flicking over the pages of a magazine in a pleasant state of inactivity.

'I was just thinking of putting on the oven,' she observed, which was palpably untrue. 'But since you're on your feet, dear, you might do it. Jeremy won't be in until late, so it's just you and me.'

Obviously Aunt Hilda had not noticed that Caroline was wet, nor that she was limping. But, like most women who enjoy a certain degree of poor health, Hilda Prentiss was totally indifferent to any distressing symptoms other than her own.

Caroline went through into the kitchen, completed the simple preparations for the evening meal already set in motion by their invaluable home help, and only then went to change into dry clothes. For some reason which she did not seek to explain to herself she still retained the ring on her finger when she returned to the dining room.

'Did you get wet?' asked her aunt, glancing out at the pouring rain.

'Yes. As a matter of fact, I fell down in a puddle.'

'Oh, dear, too bad,' was the philosophical reply. 'I myself nearly had a fall this morning. I must get Jeremy to fix that rug in my room. I was saying to Mrs Glass only yesterday that I might have a nasty fall if——' then she stopped suddenly and exclaimed, 'Where on earth did you get that ring?'

'I found it—in the Park—when I fell down.'

'You *found* it? But it's real, isn't it? Let me have a look at it.'

With an odd sense of reluctance Caroline drew the ring from her finger and handed it over.

'Yes, it's real all right.' To Caroline's annoyance, her aunt breathed on it and rubbed it on her sleeve. 'It must be worth a fortune! Why didn't you take it to the police?'

'Because I was soaking wet and I'd hurt my ankle. And anyway, I didn't know where the nearest police station was.'

'Someone's going to be dreadfully upset about losing a ring like that,' her aunt said reproachfully. 'Didn't you think about the poor owner and how she must be feeling?'

'No.' Caroline replied obstinately. 'I thought about how tired and wet *I* was, and that I would do something about the ring tomorrow.'

Her aunt clicked her tongue reprovingly.

'If it had been me I shouldn't have been able to think of anything but that poor frantic owner,' she declared. And since Caroline knew that her aunt truly believed this was so, she felt her usual good humour restored.

'Well, Auntie,' she smiled, 'I'll bestir myself

tomorrow to do everything I can to find the owner.'

Then she held out her hand firmly for the ring, which was rather reluctantly returned.

'Did you say Jeremy would be late?' she asked, anxious to change the subject.

'I expect so. He went to an evening audition.'

'He *did*?' Caroline's tired face lit up with sudden animation. An animation which changed her from a sensitive, thoughtful looking girl to a vivid, near beautiful one. 'Oh, Aunt Hilda! Something really important, do you mean?'

'He didn't say. I asked him, of course. I reminded him how it frays my nerves not to know. But he just told me to wait and see. I suppose so many disappointments have made him secretive,' she added plaintively. But then she smiled indulgently, for her son Jeremy was her idol—a point of view which Caroline completely understood.

Indeed, from the day when she had come—a scared, bewildered orphan—to make her home with Aunt Hilda and Jeremy, she had, quite simply, loved her cousin better than anyone else in the world.

She had been no more than eleven at the time, still stunned by the death of both her parents in a car crash. And Aunt Hilda, to whom family ties were of almost sacred importance, had, to her credit, unhesitatingly offered a home to her orphaned niece. If she had been to a certain extent influenced by the quite substantial inheritance which went with the niece it would be unjust to blame her. She was, after all, herself a widow living on a small pension, and Caroline and her inheritance had been most usefully absorbed into the family.

In return, she was provided with a comfortable if unpretentious home, her aunt expending upon her some degree of good-humoured affection—so long as no undue demands were made on her energies or sympathies.

Above all, Caroline was blessed by the companionship of Jeremy. He was sixteen when she joined the family, a good-natured boy with an unexpected capacity for imaginative sympathy, which prompted him to put himself out to discover ways of comforting the disconsolate child, and interesting her in various facets of her new life.

That most of these concerned himself closely was inevitable, and she became first his little confidante and then his wholehearted partner in plans for the future. His future, naturally.

Presently the years when he would inevitably leave home to go to college began to loom distressingly near. But then something wonderful happened. On the strength of a good tenor voice Jeremy obtained a grant to pursue his studies at one of London's leading music colleges. There was therefore no need for him to leave home after all—and Caroline was happy.

'It will be a long time before he earns anything like a good living,' Aunt Hilda had said, pouring unwelcome cold water on the dreams which Caroline shared with Jeremy.

'What does that matter?' Caroline had retorted stoutly. 'Families of great artists have usually had to make a few sacrifices.'

Aunt Hilda, who didn't think much of

sacrifices unless someone else was making them, replied that that was all very well, but household bills had to be paid even by the families of potentially great artists.

'We'll manage,' Caroline had declared. 'I still have a bit of my capital left. And I'll soon be earning my own living.'

So a little more was scooped out of the diminishing capital, and presently Caroline was indeed earning her living, as secretary to Kennedy Marshall, an up-and-coming musical agent. She regarded this appointment as a gift straight from an understanding Providence, for what could be more helpful to a budding tenor's future than a good agent somewhere in the background?

Things did not, however, work out quite as she had hoped. At first she was a good deal frightened by her employer, who had a quick temper which he usually—but by no means invariably—kept in check. People who liked him described him as dynamic; those who did not said he was arrogant. Both, however, had to admit that he possessed to an unusual degree that curious blend of artistic vision and business acumen which tends to make the highly successful agent in the world of music and the theatre.

To Caroline the astonishing thing about him was his vitality—a vitality which seemed to show even in the waves of his strong, almost black hair. Living, as she did, with the completely negative Aunt Hilda and the charming but less than forceful Jeremy, she had never before come in contact with such a positive human force. It was like meeting with a strong wind on a brilliantly sunny day, and it was both intimidating and oddly invigorating.

Although he was a big man there was a sort of animal grace about him, very noticeable in his quick but always purposeful movements; and Caroline, who was apt to notice people's eyes and hands, was sometimes surprised by the changing expression of the former and the unusually good shape of the latter.

She gathered that he was satisfied with her work, but most of their conversation remained on a strictly business level. He shouted at her sometimes, but occasionally apologised later, and on very rare occasions would praise her work with a sudden flashing smile which warmed her heart.

Altogether, however, it was more than six months before she ventured to inform him that she had a very gifted cousin who sang.

'Most people have,' was the discouraging reply. 'What is she? Coloratura soprano? They tend to be—or to think they are.'

'No, no. He's a tenor,' Caroline hastened to assure him.

Kennedy Marshall pulled a face at that and said. 'Even worse! You would hardly believe the number of forced-up baritones who expect me to get them leading positions as tenors.'

She bit back the indignant retort that Jeremy was a real tenor—which in point of fact he was—but the effort made her look flustered and self-conscious.

'Well?' He tipped back his chair and regarded her with a sort of exasperated amusement and said. 'You'd better make the whole confession. I suppose this is all leading up to the announcement that you yourself have singing aspirations?'

'Oh, no!' exclaimed Caroline. Then she blushed scarlet, for she was by nature a truthful girl. 'At least——'

'Yes?' He smothered a yawn and reached for a file.

'Nothing,' she told him rather haughtily, and she turned away to the filing cabinet, unaware that he regarded the back of her well-shaped head with a touch of amused curiosity.

In asserting that there was no more to admit Caroline believed she was stating no less than the truth. In the strict sense of the term she had no urgent singing aspirations. She had a voice, it was true, an unusually lovely one. But she hardly presumed to think of herself with a professional career. That was *Jeremy's* part. He it was who was destined to bring fame and fortune to the family. His was the career which was to be nurtured, guided and finally presented to an admiring world.

To enter into competition with him as he struggled up the first rungs of the ladder of fame would be base disloyalty, and no one felt that more keenly than Caroline. Consequently, it had been agreed between them during the last year or two that there was no room for more than one voice in their family.

'Even one first-class voice in an ordinary family strains most people's credulity,' Jeremy had explained. 'Two would sound totally bogus. Once I'm established, of course, I'll help you along—I promise that. But at your age you can afford to wait a bit, whereas I can't. You do agree, don't you?'

Naturally she had agreed, and even at home she spoke very little about her own singing lessons. They were in any case not very distinguished. Nothing to do with any music college—just twice a week with the seventy-year-old Miss Naomi Curtis, who had been in musical comedy in her youth. But the fact is that in Miss Curtis's youth a pretty well based technique was required in order to sing even in musical comedy—a stroke of good fortune of which Caroline was quite unaware at this point.

'I suppose you want me to hear this cousin of yours?' Kennedy Marshall suddenly broke in again on Caroline's thoughts.

'*Would* you?' She turned upon him such a dazzling smile that he blinked slightly.

'No. At least, not here and now,' he countered rather disagreeably. 'One of these days, maybe, but at the moment I've got other things on my plate. I suppose now is as good a time as any to tell you. The fact is we have a merger going through in the near future, Caroline.' He only called her Caroline when he was in a good mood. 'It will be with Dermot Deane.'

'*The* Dermot Deane?'

'I'm sure he would regard that as the right way of putting it,' her employer grinned almost boyishly.

'But he handles all the top people, doesn't he? He has done for years.'

'That's the rub for poor old Dermot—"he has done for years". He's getting on a bit now and finds the continual travelling and the strain of managing what you call the top people rather more than he can take. He had a heart attack some months ago, and though he made a good recovery his doctors told him he must ease up a bit unless he wanted more serious trouble.'

'And he chose to merge with *our* company?'

'I think he would prefer to describe it as absorbing *us* into *his* company,' her employer corrected her. 'Anyway, he needed a partner with the kind of energy and vitality which he himself once had.'

'You, in fact?' Caroline smiled back at her employer with a sort of naïve satisfaction which evidently amused him.

'It seems so,' he agreed, with an air of modesty which was almost totally spurious.

'Does that mean that *you* will be handling people like Torelli—and Nicholas Brenner, and Oscar Warrender?'

'Could be. The transfer will be a delicate one, and we shall need all our diplomacy and tact.' She thought it was nice of him to say "we", until he went on. 'So don't try to push your singing relatives into the picture, will you? I'll listen to the budding tenor one of these days, but *I* will say when.'

'Of course,' she had said rather stiffly. But she had found it difficult to explain to Jeremy why it was that month succeeded month and yet her employer—in spite of the rapid rise in his own circumstances—never suggested again that he should hear what he had referred to so slightingly as her 'singing relatives'.

The struggle to get a first foothold in the musical world can be a heartbreaking one, and Jeremy's natural good spirits were often clouded nowadays. Even when he came in that particular evening Caroline could see at a glance that he was profoundly depressed. The audition had gone quite well—but the engagement had gone to someone else.

'That's always the way,' he said dejectedly. 'I can't help knowing I was quite a lot better than the other chap who got the job. But he was already known to them, and these smaller touring companies tend to play safe and use someone whose work they've found satisfactory before. You can't blame them, I suppose, but——' he shrugged and made an unsuccessful attempt to smile.

Caroline's heart ached for him and she wished passionately that she could have had some good news for him. Why had she not made another attempt to interest her employer? It was silly and cowardly to hold back just because she knew that in these recent months of tension his temper had become unpredictable. Tomorrow, she promised herself, tomorrow she would tackle him.

At that moment her aunt's voice broke in with something as near to excitement as she could achieve.

'What *do* you think? Caroline found a perfectly wonderful diamond ring in St James's Park! Show it to him, Caroline,' she urged, as though even Jeremy's depression must give way before the sight of the splendid ring.

He took it quite indifferently, however, and all he said was, 'That's pretty. Not real, of course.'

'It most certainly is,' retorted his mother. 'I know a diamond when I see one.'

'But—that size?' Jeremy shook his head sceptically. 'It would be worth a fortune if it were real. Where did you find it, Carrie?'

Caroline explained all over again and, unlike his mother, Jeremy immediately asked if she had hurt herself when she fell.

'Not much. I'm all right now.' She smiled gratefully, for a little sympathy was welcome after Aunt Hilda's stoical indifference. 'I'll go to the police tomorrow. Or I suppose there might be an advertisment about it in the morning paper.'

'Why not the evening paper? I've got one somewhere.'

Jeremy went out into the hall and returned with a rather crumpled newspaper in his hand. He turned over the pages absently, his thoughts quite obviously more on his own affairs.

'Here we are——"Lost and Found". Now then—— "Small fawn Peke——" No, that's no good. "Dark blue wallet——" What a hope! Why—' he sat up suddenly and his voice sharpened'——here it is, by Jove! "Single stone diamond ring, lost between Victoria and Piccadilly——" Pretty wide field, that, but it could take in St James's Park all right. "Finder p'ease contact Didcot & Didcot, Solicitors, etc, for reward. Or telephone information 444–6723." That's your ring, Carrie! Then it *is* real.'

'I said it was,' declared Aunt Hilda complacently. 'I knew I couldn't be mistaken.'

'What was that phone number?' Caroline asked in a curiously breathless voice, and Jeremy repeated it.

'You could phone now,' remarked Aunt Hilda, but Caroline shook her head with sudden obstinacy, for the most extraordinary conviction had come to her that she *knew* that number. She had, for some reason, had to note it at the office recently and, if she were not mistaken, it was an important number.

Aunt Hilda was saying again that she should telephone at once, and was a good deal annoyed when Caroline replied mutinously that it was too late.

'It's never too late to give news of a lost diamond ring,' stated Aunt Hilda, and it must be admitted that she had a point there.

It was Jeremy who said peaceably, 'Leave it until the morning if you'd rather, Carrie. It could be just an office number, and no one would be there at this time of night.'

'More likely to be the owner's private number,' insisted Aunt Hilda. 'Just think of that poor woman lying awake all night. Now if it were me——'

'But it isn't, Aunt Hilda,' cut in Caroline crisply. 'Anyway, I'm going to bed now.' And she went.

Fortunately Aunt Hilda's delicate constitution required that she breakfasted late, so Caroline escaped to the office the next morning without further discussion. By now she had come to the conclusion that she had simply imagined the significance of that number. But, all the same, when she arrived at the office and found her employer already there, she took a slip of paper from her handbag and put it down on the desk in front of him.

'Do you happen to know that telephone number?' she asked casually.

'Yes, of course,' he replied without hesitation. 'It's Oscar Warrender's ex-directory number. Why?'

'It was given in a "Lost and Found" advertisment in the evening paper—about a diamond ring.'

'Really?' He looked mildly interested. 'Something of Anthea Warrender's, I suppose.'

'I suppose so—I found it. There it is.' And this time it was the ring which she laid on the desk in front of him.

'Well, I'll be—Where did you find it?'

'On the grass beside a path in St James's Park. I fell down, and just as I was scrambling up again—there it was, looking like a drop of rain, only more valuable.'

'I'll say it was!' With an intrigued smile he turned the ring in his hand, watching the way the diamond flashed in the sunlight. 'Could be her engagement ring, I suppose. Even Warrender wouldn't give a ring like that except for a special occasion, I imagine. Are you going to return it in person?'

'I—I thought of doing so—yes.'

There was a slight pause, and then she added rather shortly, 'Have you any objection?'

'I? No, not in principle. Just remember that you're not only a private person. You represent this firm. Be tactful—about the reward, for instance.'

Caroline tilted her chin angrily and said almost disdainfully, 'I do know how to behave, you know. And I didn't learn that in this office, I might add.'

Then, as she stalked to the door, she heard him laugh as he called after her, 'I'm sorry—I apologise. But, above all, don't try to foist that cousin of yours on Warrender, of all people.'

She checked very slightly in her lofty exit, then walked on, out of his office and across the passage to her own room. There she sat down at her desk and stared in front of her, her chaotic thoughts of the previous night suddenly falling into a clear and almost inevitable pattern.

It was his own fault, she told herself afterwards. It was he himself who had put the idea into words, wasn't it? She might not have thought of it on her own. At least——

She took the cover from her typewriter and rather deliberately started on the morning's work. Only when she heard her employer leaving his office and then slamming the main door behind him did she pause in her typing. She gave him ten minutes longer, then, when he had not returned, she reached for the telephone and deliberately dialled the Warrenders' number.

Almost immediately a woman's charmingly pitched voice answered. And when Caroline asked if she might speak to Lady Warrender she was not really surprised to receive the reply, 'Yes, I'm speaking.'

'Oh, Lady Warrender——' Caroline was suddenly breathless'—my name's Caroline Bagshot, and I think I've found your ring. It was——'

'You *have*? Oh, how wonderful!' The voice at the other end broke slightly and then Caroline heard her call to someone else, 'Oscar! Some darling girl has found my ring!—Where?—I don't know——' and then to Caroline, 'Where did you find it, dear?'

Caroline explained yet again about finding the ring when she fell down and, to her surprise, the celebrated Anthea Warrender (a prima donna in her own right, after all!) asked, just like kind Jeremy, if she had hurt herself.

'Not much, really. Anyway, I don't mind, because if I hadn't fallen I wouldn't have seen the ring. Lady Warrender, could I—could I *bring* your ring to you? It sounds silly, but I'd like to see your face when I hand it back.'

'Why, of course. And I don't think it's silly at all. I think it's very sweet of you to be so concerned. Shall I send the car for you?'

'Oh, no thank you! You're at Killigrew Mansions, aren't you? If I might come on my way home from the office——?'

'Yes. What time?'

'I'd be there between half past five and six.'

'Then your office can't be very far away.'

'No, it isn't,' said Caroline. And only when she had rung off did she admit to herself that—by accident or intent?—she had not mentioned where she worked.

To her relief, Kennedy Marshall was out of the office for most of the day. Then he came in late in the afternoon and she was kept busy until the last minute typing some urgent letters. She hoped and thought that perhaps he had forgotten all about the diamond ring, but just as she was leaving he said rather provocatively, 'Going to collect your reward?'

'Just so,' she replied with a cool little smile, and she took herself off to Killigrew Mansions, where her timid knock at the Warrenders' door was answered almost immediately by Anthea Warrender herself.

Caroline recognised her at once, not only from

photographs but from having seen and heard her as soloist at several concerts conducted by her famous husband.

'Come in.' She smiled radiantly. 'You're Caroline Bagshot, aren't you?—and you *really* have my ring?'

'Yes, indeed.' Caroline held it out to her even before she had been ushered into a large, pleasant studio overlooking the Park.

'Oh, my dear—thank you!' There were actually tears in Anthea's eyes as she took the ring and slipped it on her finger. 'It's my engagement ring, and I wouldn't have lost it for the world. It had been getting a little loose; it served me right for not having it attended to. I must have pulled off my glove for some reason—though I don't remember doing so—and it wasn't until I got home that I found my ring had gone. I was shattered! My husband said he would replace it with one as near as possible to the original, but that wouldn't be the same thing, would it?'

'I suppose it wouldn't.' Caroline smiled back at her rather shyly. 'I'm so very glad I found it, and I'm only sorry I didn't phone you last night.'

'It doesn't matter. Nothing matters now that I have my ring back,' Anthea assured her. 'Did we mention the amount of the reward in that particular advertisement? And would you like it as a cheque right away?'

'Lady Warrender, I don't want a reward. I mean—not a money reward. You see——'

'But of course you must have the reward! You've earned it.'

'I haven't really *earned* anything,' Caroline

replied very exactly. 'It was just luck, really. But——'

'All right. It was my luck that you found it, and your luck too, and you must have the reward.'

'Lady Warrender, when I said I didn't want the reward, I meant—not money.' Caroline was speaking rather quickly now. 'But I do want something which probably only you can arrange. That was my luck, if you like. I have a cousin—a very dear cousin—and he has a splendid tenor voice and is finding it very hard to get started. Do you—do you think you could persuade your husband to hear him and—and perhaps put in a word for him in the right quarter?'

Anthea Warrender looked slightly taken aback. Then she said slowly,

'Well, I expect he would hear your cousin, in the circumstances. But I must warn you, my dear, that nothing on earth would make him give a favourable opinion unless he felt it was deserved. Still less would he give a recommendation in any quarter unless he really thought the young man merited it. He couldn't, you know,' she said simply. 'He's not that kind of person.'

'I do understand that,' Caroline assured her earnestly. 'But if—if he would *hear* Jeremy and give his opinion. It would either be the most wonderful encouragement or—or save him from a lot of future disappointment.'

'Well, shall we ask Sir Oscar?' Anthea gave that quick smile and, getting up, she went to the door and called, 'Darling, would you come here a minute?'

He came immediately and, as he entered,

Caroline realised that he was just as overwhelming in a room as he had seemed at the Festival Hall conducting an orchestra. More so, if anything, for great personalities tend to dwarf any ordinary surroundings.

'This is Miss Bagshot,' Anthea explained. 'She's just brought back my ring.'

Warrender in his turn thanked Caroline with some charm for having restored the ring which meant so much to his wife.

'To us both, of course,' he added frankly. 'It was her engagement ring.'

'So she told me,' Caroline said shyly. 'I'm so glad it was found.'

'Miss Bagshot is not much interested in the offered reward,' Anthea explained. 'Though of course I shan't let it go at that. She has a favour to ask. You see——'

'She has a voice and wants me to hear her,' finished Sir Oscar, a faint shade of boredom coming over his handsome face.

Caroline drew in her breath in astonishment, but Anthea went on calmly, 'Not exactly. She has a cousin with a tenor voice.'

'Same thing—by one remove,' commented her husband. 'When would you like me to hear him, Miss Bagshot?'

'You mean you *will*?' Caroline's voice ran up excitedly and a sudden smile irradiated her face.

'It would be rather churlish to refuse such a modest request when you've just given my wife such pleasure,' returned Oscar Warrender, and he smiled slightly in his turn. 'But I must warn you——'

'I've already warned her, dear,' cut in Anthea

equably. 'She knows you can't—and would not—do anything unless the young man is really worthy.'

'To which I must add,' Warrender told Caroline bluntly, 'that for every worthwhile singer I have to hear, at least two dozen are no good at all, professionally speaking. Is tomorrow evening at six-thirty all right?'

'Indeed, indeed it is!' Caroline clasped her hands together in joy. 'And I can't thank you enough, Sir Oscar.'

'Don't try,' was the rather grim reply. 'You'll probably hate me by seven-fifteen tomorrow evening.' And with a slight but expressive gesture of his hand he turned and went.

'Well, that's settled!' Anthea gave her friendly smile. 'And we'll expect you both tomorrow evening at six-thirty. What's the cousin's name, by the way?'

'Jeremy Prentiss. And—and he really is good.'

'We'll hope so, anyway,' replied Anthea, and it sounded as though she really meant that.

It seemed to Caroline that the journey home had never taken so long. The bus simply crawled, stopping at every traffic light and request stop, while her excited hopes and fears ran on ahead. Suppose Jeremy were out?—perhaps for the whole evening. Could she possibly put off Aunt Hilda with just a partial account of what had happened?

By the time she reached home she was in a fever. But she had arranged in her own mind exactly what she was going to say—how she would calmly give every detail leading up to the stunning dénouement of her story. But when it came to the point, she was so relieved to hear Jeremy's voice talking to her aunt that she just rushed into the room, confronted the two of them and gasped out,

'I returned the ring. It belonged to Anthea Warrender. And he—Oscar Warrender—is going to audition you tomorrow evening, Jeremy, and give you his advice!'

Then she sat down and burst into excited tears.

'Caroline!' Actually white with joyous shock, Jeremy seized her up in his arms and exclaimed, 'Don't cry, darling! Do you mean what you're saying? Oh, my God—I can't believe it! Warrender? How on earth did you do it?'

'I just asked him and he said "yes",' gulped Caroline.

'Will someone tell me what all this fuss is about?' interjected Aunt Hilda. 'Stop crying, Caroline—my nerves won't stand it. You returned the ring, you say? What reward did they give you?'

'*That* was the reward!' Caroline raised a flushed and tear-stained face from her cousin's shoulder. 'The Warrender audition. That was what I asked for.'

'You blessed little angel!' That was Jeremy. But his mother exclaimed,

'You must be mad! That ring was worth I don't know *what*. And you're telling me they were mean enough to fob you off with the promise of an *audition*?'

'They weren't mean at all.' Caroline was calmer now. 'In fact—I remember—Lady Warrender said I would have to have something else besides the audition.'

'Well, thank heaven for that!' Aunt Hilda actually fanned herself with the magazine she had been reading. 'You gave me such a fright! My heart's still pounding. Now pull yourself together and tell us the whole story.'

So Caroline pulled herself together and gave a fairly coherent account of her incredible day, while Jeremy stood beside her, holding her hand so tightly that it was quite numb by the time he released her.

At the end he said, 'Caroline, I—I'll never forget this.' And she loved him more than ever because there was that unusual quiver in his voice.

Even Aunt Hilda said, 'You know, I could do with a drink. See if there's any sherry left, Caroline.'

'Not *sherry*,' exclaimed Jeremy. 'Not for an occasion like this. This calls for champagne. I'll go along to the corner shop and get a bottle while you and Caroline set the supper, Mother.'

'What a splendid idea,' agreed his mother, who was not of course committing herself to sharing the preparations for supper. But neither Jeremy nor Caroline cared. They were riding the topmost waves of hope and excitement, and the world was theirs that night.

The next day Caroline had some nervous tremors on the way to the office. If her employer started asking questions she must somehow manage to prevaricate until the all-important audition that evening was over. And prevaricating was not at all easy when one was face to face with Kennedy Marshall.

However, it so happened that he was lunching

with a recent and most prestigious addition to his list of artists, and had little time to enquire about his secretary's affairs. Indeed, when he returned to the office late in the afternoon Caroline detected signs of something like excitement in his demeanour, and she asked with genuine interest, 'Is this Lucille Duparc as glamorous as people say?'

'Glamorous?—No, nothing quite as obvious as that.' He smiled reflectively. 'There's something slightly enigmatic about her, both as an artist and a person. I think it's a quality more attractive to men than women. My godmother, for instance, pretends she sees nothing in her. But you must see and hear her for yourself on Thursday next.'

Caroline, who had never thought of a god-mother in connection with her employer and found some difficulty in doing so now, said that she would certainly hear Lucille Duparc.

'I'll get a ticket on the way home,' she started to say, then stopped, suddenly remembering there would be no time to run after tickets on the way home. Only just enough time to meet Jeremy and accompany him to the Warrenders' apart-ment.

But her employer seemed not to notice the sudden check. He said, 'You won't get anything now, I'm afraid. The place is sold out. Wait a minute——' He jerked open a drawer in his desk, picked out a small bundle of tickets and ran his thumb through them. 'There you are——' he tossed one across the desk to her'—and don't lose it. The ticket touts are out in force.'

'I'll take great care of it,' she promised fervently. 'And thank you very much.'

'All part of the education of an impresario's secretary,' he assured her with a grin. 'How did you get on with Anthea Warrender, by the way?'

'Very well. She was absolutely charming, and so happy to have her ring back.'

'I bet she was. And what about him? Did you meet the great Sir Oscar?'

'Oh, yes.' With a tremendous effort Caroline kept her voice steady. 'He was very nice to me too, and said the ring meant a lot to both of them because it was—as you guessed—her engagement ring.'

'Sealed one of the great love stories of the operatic world, as one might say.' He looked rather cynically amused, and then was obviously going to ask another leading question when— perhaps in answer to a silent but frantic prayer from Caroline—the telephone bell rang with blessed insistence, and, as he lifted the receiver, she fled to the safety of her own office.

The real moment of danger was past, it seemed, for he made no further reference to her encounter with the Warrenders during the rest of that afternoon, and she was able to leave in good time for her meeting with Jeremy at a coffee bar near Piccadilly.

He joined her two minutes after she had found a vacant table, but he looked pale and nervous, and when she asked him if he would like a coffee, he shook his head.

'Are you feeling a bit sick?' she enquired sympathetically.

'Yes. Are you?'

She nodded, and was aware of a chilling drop in her spirits. The possibility that they might, after all, be heading for a ghastly disappointment suddenly pierced her consciousness like a blunt knife. Until that moment she had resolutely refused to entertain any thought which was not hopeful. Now, as she looked across at Jeremy, she realised that with him also confidence was draining away by the minute.

'We'd better go,' she said huskily at last. And in complete silence they made their way to Killigrew Mansions, up in the lift to the fourth floor, and into the studio where so many before them had been tested—and probably been found wanting.

They must have looked a rather desperate couple, Caroline thought, for Oscar Warrender, who was already there waiting for them, said, 'There's no need to be scared. It's usually easier to perform for a knowledgeable audience than an ignorant one.'

'It's just that so much depends on it,' Caroline thought, while Jeremy's strained smile showed that he was thinking much the same.

Then Anthea came in, greeted Jeremy pleasantly and again told Caroline how happy she was to have her ring back. The preliminaries thus disposed of, Oscar Warrender sat down at the piano and without—to Caroline's surprise— asking Jeremy anything about his training or experience, said,

'What are you going to sing for me? Choose something in which you feel comfortable. If it's anything I know I'll accompany you. If not, I'll pick it up as we go along.'

'I'd like to sing the first act aria from "The Pearl Fishers",' replied Jeremy boldly.

'Hm—brave fellow,' commented Warrender, but not unkindly, and he began the introduction to that most lovely—and difficult—aria.

To Caroline's unspeakable horror, Jeremy went hoarse on the third bar, cleared his throat nervously and then came to a ragged halt.

'Don't worry,' said the conductor calmly. 'That can happen to anyone, particularly anyone who is nervous and under a strain. Go back and start again. Stand where I can see you.'

So Jeremy shifted his position, looked rather desperately at the man at the piano and received such a compelling nod of encouragement that he made a perfect entry and then went on confidently to the last soft high note, which he took faultlessly.

'Not bad,' observed Warrender, at which Jeremy drew a long sigh of unspeakable relief. 'But you're attempting things beyond your present capacity. Sing me a scale.'

Jeremy sang a scale, and then followed firmly and intelligently as Warrender took him further and further to the top of his natural range.

'Yes, it's a good healthy voice,' was Warrender's rather moderate verdict. 'Tell me— do you want to sing more than anything else in the world?'

Jeremy nodded wordlessly.

'Well, the future depends primarily on you yourself and your capacity to work. I don't need to tell you that the profession is a crowded one. Crowded, that is to say, by worthy mediocrities who think the world owes them an interesting living. They're wrong, of course. The world owes no one anything but what they can achieve by their own talent and hard work. Also a little bit of luck is a fine thing.'

'I regarded this audition as my bit of luck,' Jeremy said with his very engaging smile. 'And I would like to thank you for providing that. I do understand that there's no easy answer to what I'm trying to achieve, but I would just like to know if, in your opinion, I might have a chance of doing something worthwhile one day.'

'You want me to give you the unvarnished truth, I take it?'

'Yes, please.' Though Jeremy bit his lip anxiously, and Caroline found that she was digging her nails into the palms of her hands.

'Well, Jeremy—that's your name, isn't it? I doubt if there will ever be a time when the leading opera houses of the world will be competing for your services. But, if you have intelligence and a capacity for hard work to match your natural talent, you could well make a good solid career of considerable satisfaction to yourself. You *might* go even further than that, given some favourable circumstances, but it would be no kindness on may part to raise your hopes too high at this stage.'

'I see.' Jeremy looked rather serious, but not dejected.

'Sing me something else.' Warrender turned back to the piano. 'Something from the more general repertoire. These occasional specialist arias which require a very exceptional technique are seldom asked for, except from highly gifted performers who are already famous enough to have their individual requests catered for. No one is likely to put on "The Pearl Fishers" for you at this point.'

Jeremy smiled faintly and asked diffidently, 'What would you like to hear?'

'Rodolfo—the Duke in "Rigoletto"— Faust——?' suggested Oscar Warrender. 'These are the roles which are always in demand, and although you're not ready for any of them yet, you can keep them in mind.'

'Faust,' said Jeremy. 'I could sing the aria from the Garden Scene.'

'Let's try it. You couldn't do better,' Sir Oscar told him. 'No one ever wrote more felicitously for the voice than Gounod.'

So Jeremy, both challenged and encouraged, proceeded to give a very good account of himself in that aria, and at the end Warrender turned and said,

'That's extremely good, you know. The aria lies beautifully for your voice. Do you know the rest of the scene?'

'Oh, yes, of course. But we need a Marguerite for that.'

'Indeed we do.' Warrender glanced across half enquiringly at his wife. But before Anthea could utter a word Caroline heard herself say excitedly,

'Let *me* sing the Marguerite! I'd like to. I'm used to singing with Jeremy. At least——' she stopped and looked both surprised and oddly guilty.

'Very well,' Sir Oscar smiled almost indulgently. 'You come and sing Marguerite. Do you want the score?'

'Oh, no, thank you.

She came and stood beside Jeremy, a streak of excited colour in her cheeks, her heart beating eagerly at the thought that it was *she* who would be giving Jeremy the opportunity to show how well he sang in concerted music.

In the last year or so they had not sung very much together, but she was able to give just the right support, the subtle blending of vocal colour which enabled Jeremy to show another facet of his undoubted talent. She hardly thought of her own part in the performance. She thought only of how best to give Jeremy a chance to shine.

Warrender let them sing right through to the end of the scene. Then again he just glanced at his wife, this time with a slight lift of his eyebrows, to which she responded with the faintest nod.

'You're quite a gifted couple, aren't you?' he said again with a touch of indulgence. 'Do you have the same teacher?'

'Oh, no!' Jeremy laughed, and explained about his grant to St Cecilia's College.

'And you, Miss Bagshot?' Warrender turned to Caroline. 'Who is your teacher?'

'Nobody at all distinguished,' Caroline explained deprecatingly. 'Nothing to do with a music college or anything like that, you know. You wouldn't have heard of her. Her name's Miss Curtis—Naomi Curtis. She was in musical comedy years ago.'

'Well, you may tell her from me—from Oscar Warrender—that she's a very good teacher indeed. Yours is a voice which has never had anything wrong done to it. It has been allowed to develop naturally. Few teachers can say as much for their pupils.'

'Oh—oh, thank you very much!' Caroline laughed in a pleased way and coloured. 'I'll tell her, certainly. She'll be very flattered.'

'And now——' Warrender glanced at his watch '—I'm afraid I must send you away. I'm expecting another visitor. Leave your names and your addresses——'

'We have the same address,' interjected Caroline happily. 'I live with my aunt, who's Jeremy's mother,' she added decorously.

'I see.' Warrender smiled slightly. 'Well, give the particulars to my wife.' Then he turned again to Jeremy and said, 'I make no specific promises, you understand. But I'll keep you in mind for anything suitable that may come my way. It may be very small at first——'

'I don't mind. I don't mind a bit!' Jeremy assured him, and he looked in a hero-worshipping way after the famous conductor as he left the room.

Meanwhile Caroline carefully supplied Lady Warrender with a note of Jeremy's name and their address and, to her surprise, received an envelope in return.

'What's this?' She turned it over, genuinely mystified.

'That's your real reward, my dear. The audition was an extra,' Anthea told her with a smile. Then, before Caroline could make any further comment, she added, 'Janet will see you out,' and indicated a discreet-looking maid who was already waiting at the door.

'Oh—thank you——' There was no time to say anything further and, aware that she was being tactfully dismissed without a chance to argue about the reward, Caroline followed Jeremy out into the hall, and a moment later the door of the apartment closed behind them.

'Oh, Jeremy——' she hugged his arm as they stood waiting for the lift together, 'it worked! I can't believe it! It worked! Aren't you thrilled?'

'Yes. Aren't you?'

'On your behalf—of course.'

'What about on your own behalf? You got a Warrender audition too, didn't you?'

'Well—yes.' It occurred to her that there was a rather curious note in his voice, and she added anxiously. 'You didn't *mind* my singing too, did you? I mean—it was a duet. You had to have a soprano too, otherwise he wouldn't have realised how well you handle the rest of that scene.'

'But *she* was prepared to sing the Marguerite if you hadn't jumped in. Didn't you realise that?'

'Oh, Jerry, I'm so sorry! Did you very much want to sing with her?'

'What ambitious tenor wouldn't?' he retorted with a vexed laugh. 'It's the sort of chance that doesn't come twice in a lifetime.' And he pushed the bell to summon the lift with rather more force than was necessary. 'Imagine being able to say one had sung with Anthea Warrender!'

'I'm so sorry,' Caroline said again, overwhelmed with remorse, and she looked so utterly contrite, as she had sometimes when she was a child, that he said, 'It doesn't matter.'

But as they stood there in silence waiting for the lift to come, she knew it did matter. And she could think of nothing to say which would ease the situation.

'This thing must have gone out of order,' Jeremy muttered crossly, and pushed the bell again.

'It's coming now,' she said pacifically as they heard the discreet purr of the lift ascending.

Then with a gentle click it arrived at their floor, the door slid smoothly open, and out stepped Kennedy Marshall.

CHAPTER TWO

FOR a moment Caroline and her employer confronted each other in stunned silence. Then Kennedy Marshall asked grimly,

'And what are you doing here, may I ask?'

'Well, I——' she swallowed, groped for some easy explanation and found none. Then, characteristically, Jeremy came to her rescue.

'I don't know who you are,' he said pleasantly, 'but I'll thank you not to take that tone to my cousin. It's not your business what we're doing here or anywhere else, but since you're obviously the inquisitive type, I don't mind telling you. I've just been auditioning for Sir Oscar Warrender. By my cousin's arrangement,' he added grandly, as he ushered Caroline into the lift before him. Then the door closed and they were borne downwards.

'Who was that impertinent oaf, for heaven's sake?' he asked as they stepped out at the ground floor.

'That,' replied Caroline despairingly, 'was my boss.' At which Jeremy whistled and then laughed aloud.

'Well, he has no right to dictate what you do out of office hours,' he said. 'You should keep him in better order.'

'He isn't the kind to keep in order,' Caroline replied with a sigh. 'That's why I never got him round to auditioning you, I suppose.'

'Auditioning *me*?—Oh, yes, of course that was once the idea, wasn't it?' Jeremy recalled casually. 'Well, we don't need him any more. We have Oscar Warrender behind us.'

'Oh, Jeremy, not exactly,' Caroline warned him with a protesting laugh, for she saw that her cousin's hopes were taking off into very high altitudes after the encouraging scene with Sir Oscar. 'He said he couldn't guarantee anything, remember. Only that——'

'I reckon he's the kind of man who's usually better than his word. Not the kind who promises the earth and then forgets your existence the moment you go out of the door.'

'Well, I think I agree there,' Caroline admitted. 'And of course you did make a splendid showing, Jerry. If only I hadn't barged in at the wrong moment,' she added remorsefully.

'Forget it—forget it,' Jeremy advised her good humouredly. '*I've* forgotten it already. I was just disappointed for a moment not to have sung with Anthea Warrender. But I'll do that one day on my own merits, I promise you. And Warrender shall conduct for us. You'll see! So smile, Carrie dear, and don't let it be said that that sour-faced boss of yours spoiled our great evening.'

She smiled then, of course, and tried to stifle the anxiety in her heart whenever she thought of facing Kennedy Marshall the next morning.

Naturally Aunt Hilda was full of congratulations on learning how the audition had gone. She was not *surprised*, she emphasised, that Sir Oscar Warrender had realised Jeremy's value. He was, after all, supposed to have excellent judgment. But she was gratified that someone had seen the

light at last. And by the end of the evening she
was pretty well deciding whom she would invite
to accompany her to Covent Garden when
Jeremy made his debut there.

'And you say you also sang for Sir Oscar,
Caroline? Wasn't that putting yourself forward a
bit, dear? I mean—it was Jeremy's evening,
wasn't it? We don't want Sir Oscar to think we
expect him to spend his time on just anybody, do
we?'

'It was all right, Mother,' Jeremy assured her.
'He didn't mind. He was in a rather—indulgent
mood, I suppose one might say. It must be rare
with him. Anyway, Caroline filled in quite
usefully in the "Faust" duet. We needed
someone for that, you know.'

Caroline thought it was generous of him not to
mention that Anthea Warrender herself might
have been willing to 'fill in quite usefully' if she
had not put herself forward, as Aunt Hilda
expressed it. So she exchanged a grateful smile
with her cousin and felt happy again, until she
thought about the morrow.

It was all very well for Jeremy to be
lighthearted about the incident, even to find an
element of comedy in it. He was not the one who
would have to face Mr Kennedy Marshall. Nor
need he entertain any feelings of guilt. It was not
he who had worked out the elaborate plot by
which Sir Oscar Warrender (that distinguished
client of her employer) had been induced to grant
the all-important audition.

That it had been on behalf of someone other
than herself really did not exonerate Caroline.
Euphoric about the finding of Anthea

Warrender's ring, she had deliberately used her
official position to do something of which she
knew her employer would disapprove.

'If he'd been more helpful, more co-operative
about giving Jeremy a break, it need not have
happened,' she told herself, trying to shift some
of the responsibility from her own shoulders to
his. But she knew she was using specious
arguments, and she despised herself for doing so.

On the way to the office next morning she
tried to buttress her courage by reminding
herself that Jeremy was right in saying it was
not Kennedy Marshall's business what she did
outside office hours. But she knew the issue
was not quite so simple as that. She had
been—she supposed 'devious' was the word—in
her planning of the Warrender audition. That
was how her employer would see it, for,
whatever his faults might be, he was, she knew,
uncompromisingly straight in his dealings with
both clients and staff.

'Well, I shall soon know,' she admitted with a
grimace as she hung up her coat in her office and
lifted the cover from her machine.

She was all too right. For before she had sat
down at her desk his bell summoned her and,
swallowing a nervous lump in her throat, she
picked up her shorthand notebook and went
across to his office.

'You needn't bother with that notebook,' he
told her without looking up. 'You're fired.'

'I'm—what?'

'You're fired. You understand the meaning of
that word, I suppose?'

'Yes, I do, you mean bully. And you ought to

be ashamed to use it to me!' Caroline was astounded to hear herself say.

'What did you call me?' He looked up then, leaned back in his chair and regarded her with an astonishment at least equal to her own.

'I called you a mean bully, and I meant it.' She was trembling now but, oddly enough, her voice was quite steady and had taken on a deep, authoritative tone. 'How dare you speak to me as though I'd stolen the petty cash? I had every right to arrange an audition with Oscar Warrender for my cousin if I chose to do so. It was out of office hours and had absolutely nothing to do with you!'

'Aren't you over-simplifying the issue?' he suggested with dangerous calm. 'It certainly had something to do with me. You were a member of my staff. A *trusted* member of my staff until yesterday,' he added, which made her wince. 'I'd taken you into my confidence about the necessity for tact and diplomacy over the handling of the recent merger and the important clients involved. Of those clients I suppose Warrender and his wife were about the most important. When this silly business about Anthea's ring happened——'

'It was not silly,' Caroline interrupted coldly. 'What you mean is that you were peeved because you had no part in it.'

There was another moment of surprised silence, and then he said, 'I don't think I know you in this mood.'

'I don't think I know myself,' she responded unhappily, and passed her hands over her face in a singularly expressive gesture of bewilderment and distress.

'Sit down,' he growled, and she dropped into her usual chair beside his desk, still clutching the notebook he had told her she would no longer require.

'Now——' he leant forward, his hands clasped in front of him on the desk, those frighteningly penetrating grey eyes fully upon her'——are you going to tell me you feel totally guiltless about the way you've behaved in this business?'

Caroline looked back at him, and then her glance fell.

'No,' she said in a much smaller voice. 'I would much rather have told you what I was going to do—but then you wouldn't have let me do it, would you?' Then, as he didn't answer that, she went on, 'I hadn't really worked it all out at first. It was you yourself who gave me the idea.'

'*I* did?'

She nodded. 'When you knew I was going to return the ring in person, you observed in a nasty, snide sort of way, "Don't try to foist that cousin of yours on Warrender, of all people." '

There was a short silence, then he said, as though he were making a not altogether welcome discovery, 'You don't much like me, do you?'

She looked away from him, but then felt compelled to look back again.

'As a matter of fact I do—usually,' she replied reluctantly. And at that he laughed suddenly, and she thought how much it changed him and how until that moment it had never occurred to her that his laugh and his smile showed more in his eyes than in any other feature.

'Even though I'm a mean bully?' he enquired.

Caroline hesitated again and then said. 'Do you want me to take that back?'

'I think I do rather.'

'Then you must also take back the terms of my dismissal,' she told him firmly.

It was he who hesitated then until, prompted by something she could not quite define, she held out her hand to him across the desk, and he took it—reluctantly at first and then in an almost painful grip.

'Did you want to dictate anything?' she asked, withdrawing her hand after a moment and turning the pages of her notebook as though anxious to return to normality.

'No. Tell me instead how the audition went,' he replied. 'Did Warrender hail your cousin as the tenor we've all been waiting for?'

'Not exactly. But why don't you ask him yourself? You might not feel you could trust me to report accurately.'

He gave her a quizzical glance at that, reached for the telephone and then, indicating the other one, said, 'Do you want to listen in on the extension?'

Caroline shook her head, much though she would have liked to hear what passed, and replied, 'No, thank you. If Sir Oscar speaks confidentially to you it wouldn't be right for me to overhear, would it?'

'I see you have your scruples—even if they don't always apply in my case,' he retorted. But he added, 'Stay where you are,' when she made a move to go.

So she stayed, and watched his face as he dialled, greeted Sir Oscar, who evidently replied in person, and then said, 'I understand you auditioned a young tenor yesterday evening?— No, I don't know him, having met him only briefly.' He grinned across at Caroline, who flushed as she recalled the scene by the lift. 'Do you mind telling me what you thought of him?'

There was a pause while presumably Warrender gave his opinion. Then Kennedy Marshall said,

'Just so—just so. What did you say?—Oh, the girl who was with him? Yes, I know her better.' Then there was quite a long pause and he began to scribble something on the pad in front of him. 'Are you sure?—Well, no, of course, I know one never can be *quite* sure. It's just that you surprise me. Yes, I know her very well. As a matter of fact she's my secretary, and is sitting in front of me at the moment.'

Caroline stirred uneasily and her employer went on, 'What's that you say?—No, of course I won't. May I tell her the gist of what you've said? With the usual warnings about high hopes, of course. Yes, naturally I'll keep an eye on her. Have you any idea who her teacher is?—Good God, you don't say!' Then he laughed and, after a few more remarks, he replaced the receiver and looked across at Caroline.

'You never told me you sang,' he said after a slight pause.

'I didn't think it was important—or would interest you.'

'Didn't you really?' He looked down at what he had written and after a moment Caroline asked diffidently,

'What did Sir Oscar say about Jeremy?—if it's not confidential.'

'No, it's not confidential. Warrender said he's a good promising lad, with an excellent voice, and that with hard work and a bit of luck he should make a satisfactory career, provided his hopes aren't too high. But then he went on——' Kennedy Marshall consulted the notes he had made '—he went on to say, "But it's the girl who interests me." '

'*Me?*' gasped Caroline.

'You. He said, "I may be mistaken, though I seldom am——" a typical bit of Warrender arrogance, of course—"but I think that girl is something quite out of the ordinary. I haven't heard such potential for a long time." '

There was quite a silence, then Caroline said, 'I don't think I can believe that.'

'True, all the same. I mean—it's true that Warrender said it. Did it never occur to you that you had a voice of some quality?'

'Occasionally—yes. I mean, I sometimes wondered. But it was *Jeremy*'s voice that mattered.'

'Are you in love with Jeremy?'

'No,' said Caroline quickly, then blushed. 'What did Sir Oscar mean by "potential", do you think?'

'Primarily the voice, of course, and then the way you use it, your attitude to what you're singing, and possibly your projection of whatever character you're depicting. Have you had any stage training, Caroline?'

'No.' She shook her head. 'Not even amateur experience. I suppose I do identify with the character. Last night it was Marguerite in "Faust". But I hadn't thought about any dramatic powers. Had you?—In connection with me, I mean.'

'Not until half an hour ago. But when you began to berate me and call me names it did rather suggest Lady Macbeth on the warpath.'

She gave a vexed little laugh and said, 'Now you're just teasing me, aren't you?'

'Not entirely. Your voice deepened and darkened as I'd never heard it do before. And when you said that nasty bit about stealing the petty cash I wouldn't have been surprised to see you produce a dagger.'

'I'm sorry. I've *said* I'm sorry.'

'All right, don't apologise again. The whole incident was most revealing and rather refreshing,' he assured her. 'You're usually so quiet and self-contained. I don't think I've ever come across anyone before who can bank down the inner fires so effectively. It's possible Warrender really did release some hidden acting talent yesterday evening. But weren't you afraid of him? Most people are.'

'Of Sir Oscar?—oh, no.'

'Only of me?'

'Well, yes. Sometimes—when you lose your temper.'

'I must tell Warrender that,' declared her employer with some satisfaction. 'To be more intimidating than Oscar Warrender is quite an achievement! Now tell me something about your teacher. She's some old girl from the great days of musical comedy, according to Warrender.'

'That isn't the way I would describe her myself,' replied Caroline rather repressively. 'Her name is Miss Curtis—Naomi Curtis. She *was* in musical comedy years ago—yes. And Sir Oscar said I was to tell her from him that she's obviously a very good teacher indeed. I'll do so tomorrow when I go for my usual Saturday lesson. She'll be delighted.'

'Could I come and hear your lesson?' Kennedy looked both amused and curious. But then, before she could say she very much doubted if Miss Curtis would agree to that, he added, 'No—I forgot—I can't. I'm taking our Lucille Duparc to lunch.'

'Again?' Caroline said that without thinking, but at a slight change in his expression she amended that hastily with, 'Not that it's my business, of course!'

'No, it isn't, is it?' he agreed drily. But, perhaps realising that he had sounded unnecessarily touchy, he reverted to the subject of her teacher and said thoughtfully, 'Naomi Curtis? The name doesn't ring a bell with me. What did she play?'

'I have no idea. It was long before my time—and yours too, I imagine. Anyway, she didn't have star roles. Hers wasn't that kind of voice. Oddly enough, what she recalls with the greatest pride is some role she had in a straight play. Quite a secondary one dramatically, I gather, but it required someone who could sing with great taste and musicality during the course of the action.'

'What was the play called?'

'I'm afraid I can't remember that.' Caroline shook her head regretfully. 'But I do remember the name of the woman who played the leading role, because Miss Curtis thought the world of her. The name was Sophie Lander.'

He gave her an odd sort of glance at that and asked drily, 'What made you pick that name out of the hat, for heaven's sake?'

Caroline looked astonished.

'It was the name Miss Curtis mentioned. It doesn't mean a thing to me. Why should it?'

'Sophie Lander was the stage name of my legendary godmother before she married old Van Kroll.'

'Your——? Oh, then you really *have* a godmother? I didn't quite believe you when you mentioned her the other day. And even now the word "legendary" seems appropriate.' Caroline laughed outright. 'You don't strike one as anyone's godchild, if I may say so.'

He laughed too then, though rather reluctantly, but he asked with real curiosity. 'What did your Miss Curtis say about her? Was she a good actress? I never saw her on the stage myself. She'd left and married Van Kroll before I was born.'

Caroline considered the question before saying slowly, 'I asked Miss Curtis that once and she made an odd reply. She said, "Not really—no. She didn't need to be. When she came on to the stage or into a room you didn't notice anyone else."'

Kennedy's laugh was quite uninhibited that time and he said, 'That's my godmother all right! As a matter of fact, she may be coming to Lucille's recital. If she does I'll introduce you to each other. She's in about the same age group as your Miss Curtis—but even so I think you'll see what I mean. And now——' he pushed a pile of correspondence towards her'—take those and attend to them. They're routine stuff. You know as well as I do what's required.'

Then he dismissed her with a peremptory wave of his hand, as though he thought they had already wasted enough time on matters of secondary importance.

Among those he evidently included Caroline and her singing capabilities, whatever Oscar Warrender might have said about her, and on the whole Caroline was now ready to agree with him.

After all, as she had said, it was *Jeremy*'s career with which they were all concerned. She wished he hadn't asked if she were in love with Jeremy, and still more did she wish she had not blushed at the question. But no one before had ever asked her to define her feelings where Jeremy was concerned. Of course she loved him. His hopes were her hopes; his ambitions, her ambitions. When she looked into the future Jeremy was always there. He had been part of her life—the most important part of it—for as long as she could remember. A future without him was simply unthinkable.

That being so, she felt presumptuous—even oddly embarrassed—at the recollection of Warrender's complimentary words about herself. As though she were more interesting vocally than Jeremy! It just wouldn't do.

'I can't tell Jeremy what Sir Oscar said,' she decided. 'I can't tell *anyone*—except perhaps Miss Curtis.'

And as she thought about Miss Curtis and all that she owed to her, Caroline made one cast-iron resolution. She would pay her much more generously for her lessons in future—out of the unexpectedly lavish reward which Anthea had given her for the return of the famous ring.

This inevitably provoked some argument with Aunt Hilda, who was always interested in matters of finance. She had evidently been thinking over the question of the reward and, on Caroline's return that evening, she asked outright if she had yet received it and how much it was.

Rather reluctantly Caroline told her.

'Well, that was very generous, I must say!' was the approving comment. 'What are you going to do with all that money? It's a very pleasant sort of subject for speculation, isn't it?'

Caroline said that it was.

'There'll be a nice present for you and for Jeremy, of course—and myself,' said Caroline, with an air of giving the matter great thought. 'Then I'll bank the rest and set some aside for my lessons with Miss Curtis. I've always felt that I don't pay her enough.'

'Miss Curtis? Why, Caroline, what an *odd* idea!' exclaimed Aunt Hilda. 'There's nothing very serious about those lessons. It isn't as though they were real professional lessons, like Jeremy's. She's just a nice elderly lady making a little bit extra while pleasing you. But don't get exaggerated ideas about yourself, dear, just because we really do happen to have a professional singer in the family. And don't start throwing your money about just because Lady Warrender was generous.'

Sorely tempted to blurt out what Sir Oscar had said about herself, Caroline held her breath and silently counted ten. And fortunately at that moment Jeremy came in—in high good humour.

'You won't believe it!' He kissed his mother—and Caroline too, which was rather unusual and indicated that he was feeling specially happy and expansive. 'But this seems to be our week for hobnobbing with the great, Carrie. You've heard of the French singer Lucille Duparc, I suppose?'

'Of course. We represent her.'

'Well, I met her today.'

'You *met* her?—Where?'

'At the French Cultural Institute. There was a midday reception for her, and some of us from the College were invited. So I went along, and got talking with her—she's charmingly easy to talk to, not a bit inclined to give herself airs—and I found myself telling her about the Warrender audition. She seemed genuinely interested, and when I told her I sang Faust's aria from the Garden Scene for him, she laughed—she has an enchanting laugh—and said maybe one day she'd sing Marguerite to my Faust. I'm going to her recital on Thursday.'

'You are? But I doubt if you'll get a ticket now,' Caroline told him regretfully. 'I myself——'

'Oh, that's all right. She gave me a ticket—on the spot,' Jeremy said casually. 'And she said I was to come round and see her afterwards. Of course there'll be dozens of people milling around, but—I don't know——' he smiled reminiscently'—I think she'll remember me all right. We got on well, somehow. We laughed a lot. Did I tell you she has a lovely laugh?'

'Yes, you did,' said Caroline, and felt unaccountably depressed.

She had been right to decide not to mention

anything Sir Oscar had said about her inconsiderable self. Perhaps even Miss Curtis would take it all casually, when it came to the point.

Miss Curtis, however, provided no such disappointment the next morning. She flushed with pleasure when Caroline reported the great conductor's comment on her own teaching powers.

'Why, Caroline,' she exclaimed, 'you must have been in splendid form to make that impression! Thank you for doing me such credit, dear. Oscar Warrender to say I was a good teacher! Just fancy that!'

'A *very* good teacher was what he said,' amended Caroline. 'And then later—though I'm not taking this too seriously—he said to my boss on the phone that I—I had very unusual potential.'

'So you have, my dear,' Miss Curtis said warmly. 'I've always thought so—only you're too much under the shadow of that cousin of yours. What did your boss—your employer—say to that?'

'I think he was as surprised as I was,' Caroline confessed. 'But he asked about you and was impressed. Oh, and—I know this sounds a bit as though I'm making it up but, you know, there *are* some occasions when surprises seem to pile on each other in the strangest way—what impressed him most was that you'd known Sophie Lander. She's his godmother.'

'His godmother? She can't be!'

'Yes, she is. Though I do agree it seems such an improbable relationship for a rather aggressive businessman. He never saw her on the stage

himself because she retired before he was born.
She must be very *old*.'

'No older than I am,' replied Miss Curtis
primly. 'She was hardly thirty when she retired.
She married a Dutch millionaire—at least, we all
thought he was a millionaire. Anyway, he was
immensely rich and insisted on her leaving the
stage on her marriage. Such a pity, because he
didn't live more than about a year after that. But
at least he left her all his money—which is always
a help.'

'She could have gone back to the stage then if
she'd wanted to, couldn't she?' said Caroline
curiously.

'I suppose she could—but she never did. I
don't think the stage meant much to her. I mean,
she wasn't a dedicated artist or anything like that.
Fancy her being anybody's godmother!' Miss
Curtis laughed reminiscently. 'Well, I suppose if
you're the widow of a millionaire parents tend to
think it would be nice to have you take an interest
in their offspring.'

'I suppose they do,' agreed Caroline with a
laugh. Then she added tentatively, 'I just might
be meeting her at a concert on Thursday. If I do
shall I mention you to her?'

'If you like.' Again Miss Curtis gave that
reminiscent little laugh. 'We got on very well
when we were young. She used to call me into her
dressing-room and we used to laugh and gossip
together. That was how I knew about Van Kroll
before anyone else did. But of course it's all years
and years ago. She wouldn't remember me now.
Not after all the important people she would have
known since.'

But Miss Curtis was quite wrong.

On the following Tuesday, in the middle of some important dictation, Kennedy Marshall said,

'Oh, I saw Sophie last night—my godmother, you know—and she remembers your Miss Curtis perfectly. She says she was a pretty, lively little thing with a great sense of fun, and that she had a lovely light soprano voice. Apparently she had lots of admirers——'

'Miss Curtis did? I can't believe it! Nowadays she's very quiet and almost mousy. Terribly nice, of course, but——'

'My dear girl, this was all about forty years ago, I suppose. We all change a bit in forty years, you know. Though you may not,' he added quite unexpectedly. 'Your facial bone structure is very good.'

'Thank you. But tell me some more about Miss Curtis. She'll be entranced to be remembered like this! She said your godmother couldn't possibly remember her after all these years and all the important people she had met.'

'It isn't always the important people one remembers, Caroline,' said her employer quite seriously. 'Anyway, they were girls together, I suppose, and apparently giggled about their respective beaux in their dressing-rooms. Your Miss Curtis was against Sophie marrying Van Kroll. She thought she was only doing it for the money—which of course she was.'

'How do you know?' countered Caroline. 'You weren't even born then—you said not.'

'Well, that's true. But why else would a lovely girl—and apparently she was a stunner—marry a man twice her age?'

'Perhaps he was very attractive. Some elderly men are.'

'Not this one. Not judging from the photographs.'

Caroline laughed and said that beauty was notoriously in the eye of the beholder. Then she added quite eagerly, 'Will she—your godmother—be at the Lucille Duparc recital, as you suggested? I'd really love to meet her after hearing so much about her.'

'Yes, I think she'll be there. I suppose we ought to have tried to get your Miss Curtis a ticket. But——' he opened the top drawer once more and took out a now much diminished pack of tickets. 'Pity—but I'm afraid all these are answered for twice over. There just are no tickets left.'

'Except with the lady herself,' murmured Caroline absently.

'Well, she's entitled to a few. But how did you know she had some?' he asked curiously.

'She gave one to my cousin Jeremy when she met him casually at a reception.'

'To a casual stranger?—that's naughty. Unless—oh, *that*'s who it was!' An amused smile broke over his face. 'I knew I'd seen him somewhere. Outside the lift, of course, when he told me to mind my own business. So it's your cousin Jeremy who's on waving terms with her, is it?'

'On waving terms?' Caroline found that she disliked the expression intensely, and her tone was sharper than she had intended. 'What do you mean exactly?'

'He was in the restaurant where I took Lucille

to lunch on Saturday, and they waved to each other very cordially, I thought. So she'd given him one of the precious tickets, had she? Fast mover, your cousin Jeremy. But I have to admit he's quite a good-looker in his own way. I didn't notice when we met head-on outside the Warrenders' apartment. But Lucille is right—he's almost too handsome for a tenor.'

'She said—that?' Caroline was divided between gratification on behalf of Jeremy and a sort of dismay for which she was quite unable to account. 'So you discussed Jeremy?'

'I wouldn't put it quite like that. She said, "You see that dark-eyed Adonis over there? He's a tenor in addition to everything else. It doesn't seen fair, does it?" And I just murmured something noncommittal, having quite enough troubles of my own without having unknown tenors wished on to me.—Let me see, where were we?'

Caroline glanced down at her notebook, read back the last paragraph with commendable accuracy, and thought, 'I'll ask Jeremy about Lucille Duparc.'

But she knew suddenly that she would not.

During the next two days Jeremy also made no reference to Lucille. But he went about looking rather pleased about something, and Caroline heard him putting in a lot of practice on a French song he had not previously tried over.

'I never heard you sing that before,' she said casually. 'It suits your voice well.'

'Think so?' He smiled as though gratified. 'I rather thought so too.'

'What made you choose it?'

There was a second's hesitation, then he said,

'Someone suggested it to me, and I thought I'd have a bash at it.'

And somehow she simply could not make herself ask who had made the suggestion. It would have been such a natural question only a few days ago. Now his once open manner had become slightly veiled as though a faint cloud had risen between them.

Caroline felt dismayed out of all proportion to the little incident, and her disquiet deepened when, on the night of the concert, he left the house half an hour before she did, without comment.

'He's going to get flowers for her, I expect,' observed Aunt Hilda complacently. 'It's his way of acknowledging her kindness in giving him a ticket. He's got something rather extravagant in mind, I imagine—he borrowed five pounds.' But she said that indulgently.

Caroline made some noncommittal reply and presently took herself off to the concert, feeling in some way rather out of things.

Although it was Lucille Duparc's first London recital she already had a considerable reputation based on her gramophone records, and when Caroline arrived at the hall the vestibule was already crowded, with at least three major critics conspicuous in the throng.

One or two cronies from the Covent Garden amphitheatre and the Festival Hall greeted her, but she managed not to become involved in any long conversations. Instead, she went almost straight to her seat, telling herself that she would rather be left on her own at the moment.

This was not, however, strictly true. She

longed for some contact with Jeremy—some confidential word perhaps about his offering to the heroine of the evening—and when she saw him come in and take his seat on the other side of the hall she felt chilled by the rather indifferent wave which was all he bestowed upon her.

Her thoughts were still deeply engaged with Jeremy when she had to stand to allow a tall, elegant woman to pass to the seat beyond hers, and was a good deal startled to be greeted with,

'You must be Ken's secretary, Caroline Bagshot.'

'Why, yes, I am.—Oh, and you must be the famous Sophie Lander,' exclaimed Caroline. 'At least—I'm sorry! I mean Mrs Van Kroll, of course.'

'Don't apologise. I haven't been called Sophie Lander for so long. It's somehow rather touching to hear it again. And now I must have a good look at you——' the older woman turned towards Caroline with uninhibited curiosity. 'Ken says your eyes are exactly the same colour as mine.'

'Really? But does he know the colour of my eyes?' Caroline was amused and faintly put out. 'We are usually too busy to——'

'Dear child, no man is ever too busy to notice a woman's eyes if they're worth noticing! And I see yours are. Ken is right—they're the same shade of violet blue as mine. It's very rare, you know,' Sophie Van Kroll added complacently.

'Is it?' Caroline was amused, but took the opportunity to look with some frankness at her employer's legendary godmother. Immediately she was aware of a sort of pleasurable shock. For even now—at seventy or whatever it was—Mrs

Van Kroll was one of the most beautiful women she had ever seen.

'If Mr Marshall was right about *me*. Miss Curtis was right about *you*,' she exclaimed.

'In what way?'

'She said that when you came on the stage or into a room no one noticed anyone else.'

'Oh, that was years ago.' The older woman laughed and shrugged. 'And Naomi was always rather prejudiced. Though I was very good-looking in my youth,' she added impersonally and entirely without conceit. 'Now tell me something about Naomi. How is she these days?'

So Caroline explained about her connection with Miss Curtis and her own singing lessons, and Mrs Van Kroll said, 'I must arrange to see her again. Just to talk about her makes me feel young and silly and irresponsible again.'

Caroline found it difficult to imagine Miss Curtis young and silly and irresponsible, but before she could say so, her companion glanced down at her programme and asked, 'Have you heard this woman?'

'No. Have you?'

'Yes. Once or twice in Paris.' Mrs Van Kroll looked critically at the photograph on the cover of the programme. A very attractive photograph of a rather appealing face. And she observed dispassionately. 'She's not a bit like that really.'

'No?' Caroline looked intrigued and amused. 'What *is* she like then?'

'Like one of those gorgeous cats who always get top rating at a cat show, because they're much to cute to sharpen their claws on any of the judges until the prizes have been awarded.'

'O-oh! That sounds rather dangerous.'

'She *is* dangerous, my dear. That sort always is. I wouldn't have her set sights on any man I was fond of—Ken, for instance,' she added reflectively as she saw her godson coming up the gangway. 'But I shall probably kiss her afterwards in the green room,' she admitted without shame. 'One does, you know.'

There was no time for Caroline to make any sort of reply to that, even if she could have thought of one. A second later her employer slipped into his seat on the other side of his godmother and Lucille Duparc made her entrance on to the platform.

The recital was destined for success from the first number, Caroline admitted to herself without reservation. The voice was warm and of an intensely individual quality, and Lucille Duparc used it with consummate skill and artistry. In contrast to that appealing manner of hers the luscious, sexy sound was extraordinarily piquant. Then, in a group of Spanish songs, just before the interval, she suddenly changed her whole manner, almost frightening Caroline with the intensity of her feeling and purpose, and bringing half the delighted audience to their feet.

'She must be tremendously effective on the operatic stage,' Caroline said to her employer, fascinated in spite of herself.

'Oh, she is,' he replied with a satisfied smile. 'Even if my godmother doesn't like her,' he added, with a faintly provocative glance at Mrs Van Kroll.

'I, my dear?' She opened those remarkable eyes in innocent surprise. 'She's a very fine artist. What makes you think I don't like her?'

'A certain pricking of my thumbs which is infallible,' he retorted, at which she gave him a quite heavenly smile and said,

'I shall go backstage afterwards to express my fervent admiration. And Caroline will come with me, won't you, dear?'

'If you'd like me to.' Caroline gave an interrogative glance at her employer, who nodded his assent.

During the interval she kept on wishing that Jeremy would come across to her and exchange at least a few words of friendly comment, but he made no move to do so. And just as she had made up her mind to take the initiative and go to him the audience began streaming back into the hall, and the interval was obviously over.

The second half of the programme was as remarkable—and as well received—as the first, Caroline finding herself almost completely under Lucille Duparc's spell by the end. Then, when all the encores had been cheered, and all the flowers presented and acknowledged with grateful, wide-eyed surprise, Caroline went round backstage with Mrs Van Kroll, her employer having slipped away ahead of them just before the last encore.

The green room was crowded and at first it was difficult to see Lucille for the admirers milling round her. But because of her extra height Caroline's companion evidently saw rather more than she did. For she suddenly said softly, 'No—I don't think I need worry about Ken.'

'*Worry* about him?' It had never occurred to Caroline that anyone need worry about her employer. To the best of her belief he was singularly well equipped to look after himself, and she said as much.

'Oh, you never know,' was the knowledgeable reply. 'Most men are fools at one time or another. But at the moment it's that good-looking young man she has in view. Lean a little this way. You can't see him where you are.'

So Caroline leaned a little towards Mrs Van Kroll, and gave a slight gasp. For the young man at whom Lucille Duparc was smiling with such compelling charm was Jeremy.

'You see?' Her companion gave a pitying shrug.

'Yes—I see,' Caroline replied, and was suddenly aware of a stab of pain that was almost physical. A pain which she bewilderedly identified as raging jealousy.

CHAPTER THREE

IT was late when Caroline reached home after the concert. Not that she had been included in any celebration supper, of course. Nor that there had been even so much as a cup of coffee and a sandwich with Jeremy, which was their usual ending to an evening after attending the same concert.

In the green room she had been briefly presented to the star of the evening by Kennedy Marshall as 'my invaluable secretary', while Jeremy stood by smiling but making no attempt to claim any connection with her. After that there was nothing to do but bid goodnight to Mrs Van Kroll (her employer had already turned away) and make her departure through the now more or less empty hall.

On the whole, Caroline tended not to join the throng waiting at the stage door after a performance, but on this occasion she did so, though she kept well to the back of the crowd. Jeremy would almost certainly come out this way, she argued, and then they would go home together, discussing the evening—as they had discussed so many evenings in their time—and everything would be as it had always been. The passionate emotion which had shaken her earlier would fade into normality.

But it had not been like that at all. She had had to wait quite a long time, alternately chilled by the slight wind which had sprung up and hot with a sort of shame that she should be standing there waiting—for what?

At last Jeremy came out. But Lucille came out with him. She even handed him some of her flowers, saying, 'Hold those for me, darling,' while she signed some eagerly proffered programmes. Then he and she entered a large waiting car and drove away, while Caroline fled from the scene before her employer and his godmother could come out and find her waiting there, ignored and ashamed.

She walked home, though she could hardly have said why. It was a long way, and there was a perfectly convenient bus if she had cared to take it. But she could not have sat still in any bus. She had to *move*—and fast, in some desperate attempt to outdistance her own thoughts. But there was no way of doing that.

'It's absurd!' she told herself. 'Why ever shouldn't Jeremy go out to supper with another woman? It's a wonderful experience for him—a struggling singer—to go with a celebrated artist. Any young man would have jumped at the chance.'

But that was not the whole of it, and well she knew it. Until tonight Jeremy and she had shared almost every experience connected with his musical development—right from the first time when as a child she had listened entranced to his practising, until the magical, undreamt-of excitement of the Warrender audition which had seemed to open up fresh vistas of hope and joy.

It would have been ungenerous to dwell on the fact that it was she alone who had engineered that

last experience for him, and she resolutely
refused to do so. She had been so *happy* to offer
him that glorious chance. In all her life she had
never been happier than when she rushed into the
house and told him that Warrender had agreed to
hear him.

'I didn't want anything in return. Not a thing.
It was so wonderful just to give him joy. Only—
only——' two big hot tears suddenly ran down
her cheeks and she caught her breath on a sob
'—if only he'd acknowledged me this evening! Just
said, "This is my cousin Caroline." Oh, it's silly
to mind, but I do mind. I do—I do! Maybe it's
ungenerous of me, but I w-wanted him to say,
"This is my cousin Caroline."'

Yet what young man was going to drag cousins
into the picture when a dazzling Lucille Duparc
was calling him 'darling' and asking him to hold
some of her floral tributes?

'It isn't as though there's anything specially
interesting or exciting about *me*,' she thought
dejectedly. 'I'm ordinary—that's what it is. I'm
ordinary. No stardust about me. Cousins don't
rate much in the stardust league. Except——'

And then she stopped dead, not a hundred
yards from her own front door. For what was it
that Oscar Warrender had said about her, if her
employer had reported correctly?

'It's the girl who interests me.'

Also something about her being 'out of the
ordinary' with 'remarkable potential'.

Her footsteps, which had been dragging
wearily, suddenly quickened, and she reached the
house almost at a run.

Predictably Aunt Hilda called out, 'Is that you,

Caroline?' as soon as she stepped into the hall, but her voice came rather sleepily from her bedroom, and Caroline had only to reply,

'Yes, Auntie. I'll tell you all about it in the morning.'

'Is Jeremy with you?'

Her throat ached suddenly, but she managed to reply quite steadily, 'No. He—went out to supper with someone. I'll leave him to slip the front door bolt when he comes in. Good night.'

Then she went into the kitchen, helped herself to a glass of milk and a biscuit and stood there sunk in thought while she absently consumed them. After that she went to her own room and, without even taking off her coat, sat down before the dressing table and examined her reflection in the mirror with more intensity than she had ever bestowed on herself before.

It's the girl who interests me.

But why? Why should Sir Oscar Warrender, who was, by his own cynical admission, pestered by would-be stage performers, be interested in Caroline Bagshot, hitherto little more than an admiring supporter for her cousin Jeremy?

The violet-blue eyes on which Mrs Van Kroll had commented so favourably stared back at her out of a rather anxious face. Then, quite deliberately, she smiled—and was surprised to see how subtly that changed her whole appearance.

Still without taking her eyes from the girl reflected back at her, she put up her hands, loosened the chestnut-coloured hair and, with a quick shake of her head, brought the gleaming waves into a softer frame around her face.

'Not bad,' she said aloud. 'Good enough to team up with a voice which could interest Oscar Warrender. It's the voice that matters, not the face.'

But that voice would have to be developed, burnished, brought to full beauty. And—how?—how?

At that moment she heard Jeremy open the front door.

He came straight to her room, knocked softly and asked in a half-whisper, 'Are you asleep, Carrie?'

'Almost.' She gave a realistic little yawn.

'Oh——' He was disappointed, she could hear that from the tone of his voice. But she didn't care. For the first time in her life she simply did not *care* that she had disappointed him and brought that note of protest from him.

Then, in the same excited whisper, he said, 'What did you think of Lucille? Wasn't she gorgeous?'

'Absolutely wonderful,' replied Caroline, making a slight face at herself in the mirror. 'We'll have to talk about her tomorrow.' Another yawn.

'Indeed we will,' he agreed. 'Good night.'

'Good night,' she returned. And she went on sitting there smiling faintly at herself in the mirror and thinking, 'I *pretended*. How odd. I never pretended anything to Jeremy before.'

She continued to pretend the next morning during the hurried breakfast he and she shared. There was little she needed to say, however. All Jeremy wanted was to give an uninterrupted account of the wonderful time he had had at the supper party the previous evening, and he looked genuinely taken aback when she interrupted drily with,

'I was a little surprised that you didn't introduce me when I came backstage.'

'Introduce you? Wasn't that for your boss to do if he felt it necessary?'

'Not really—no. He's not related to me, and you are. You were standing by when I said my few words of congratulation. Didn't it even occur to you to say, "This is my cousin Caroline"?'

'Frankly, no. It might have seemed to Lucille that I was trying to include you in the supper party,' he said rather naïvely.

'I see. Well, tell me some more about this party.'

'I wasn't the only one there, of course. I mean—it wasn't what you might call an intimate affair. But she insisted on my sitting beside her.' Jeremy was back on course again after that slight interruption, and laughed with such transparent satisfaction that she was curiously touched and almost reduced to her old role of absorbed listener.

'It was rather one in the eye for that self-satisfied boss of yours, I imagine. He was there, of course—with a handsome woman old enough to be his grandmother.'

'His godmother,' amended Caroline. 'Mrs Van Kroll.'

'Was that who it was? No wonder he paid a good deal of attention to her! She's pretty well-heeled, isn't she?'

'I don't know,' said Caroline, coldly and untruthfully. 'But that wouldn't be the only consideration. He isn't at all mercenary.'

'How do you know?' asked Jeremy, not unnaturally.

'I just do know,' she insisted. 'But tell me some more about Lucille Duparc.'

So he told her some more about Lucille Duparc, a good deal of it rather repetitive, until she said she must fly or she would be late. On this they parted, he obviously believing that they shared a common admiration for the French soprano.

It promised to be a fairly slack day for Caroline as her employer was making a brief visit to Paris to engineer a couple of important contracts. She dealt rapidly and efficiently with the post, and completed an unfinished task left over from the previous day. Then, after some thought, she deliberately rolled a sheet of paper into her typewriter and began:

'Dear Sir Oscar, I hope you will not think I'm presuming on the kindness you've already shown me, but my employer, Mr Kennedy Marshall, has told me that you spoke well of my vocal potential, so far as you could assess it the other evening.

'My problem is that, apart from my voice teacher, I have no one who can advise me about what I should do to develop further any talents I may possess. Would you be willing to give me the name of someone I might consult for further guidance?

'I should be deeply grateful if you could do so. On the other hand, I should fully understand if you felt that I should take my personal problems to someone less distinguished than yourself. Yours sincerely—Caroline Bagshot.'

She read it over three times, with less satisfaction each time. To battle for Jeremy had become second nature to her. But to battle on her own behalf was something so completely new to her that she found herself in unknown country, with some doubt about every step she took.

If she had not recalled the words, 'It's the girl who interests me,' she would probably have torn up the letter at that point. Instead, she put it into an envelope, addressed it to Sir Oscar Warrender at Killigrew Mansions, and took it with her when she went out to lunch.

Ignoring two postboxes which she passed, she took it in person to the elegant block of flats in St James's and handed it to the porter in the entrance hall. Then she walked rapidly away before the last grain of courage could desert her.

She presumed he would reply—if he replied at all—by post. But, back in the office, the horrid thought came to her that perhaps two short sentences on the telephone might be a more characteristic way of dealing with a presumptuous request from a virtual stranger.

'If only Mr Marshall hadn't rushed off to Paris,' was the rather unfair reflection which followed on that. 'He'd have kept me too busy to do anything so ill-judged as pester Sir Oscar. *Putting myself forward*, as Aunt Hilda's horrid phrase has it!'

And then the telephone rang and, with an unsteady hand, she picked up the receiver, already rehearsing her apologies to Sir Oscar.

It was not, however, Sir Oscar who spoke. It was her employer, calling from Paris to request some necessary information. Caroline supplied this promptly, but there must have been something unusual in her voice, because, having dealt with the matter, he suddenly asked, 'Are you all right?'

'All right?—Yes, of course. Why not?'

'You didn't sound exactly yourself somehow. Must be the phone. Oh, by the way, you made quite a hit with my rather exacting godmother.'

'*Did* I?' Caroline was inordinately pleased by this much-needed boost to her morale. 'Thank you very much.'

'Don't mention it. It's a pleasure to transmit compliments between two charming women,' he retorted with a laugh. 'It doesn't happen all that often in our world.' And, still laughing, he rang off.

In some way she felt better for having heard his voice, and, since the rest of the afternoon passed without incident, her agitation had quieted by the time she gathered her things together to go home. Then, just as she reached the door, the telephone rang again.

Reluctantly she returned to pick up the receiver once more, and a precise female voice said, 'May I speak to Miss Bagshot, please?'

'This is Miss Bagshot,' replied Caroline, swallowing a slight lump in her throat.

'I have a message from Sir Oscar Warrender,' went on the precise voice. 'If you will come to Killigrew Mansions at six o'clock this evening, he will see you then.'

'Oh, thank you,' gasped Caroline, and then, as her caller rang off, she dropped into her chair, trying to decide if that curt reply, through a second party, meant that she was to receive valuable information or what might be best described as the complete brush-off.

'No, he wouldn't have bothered to see me if he meant to brush me off,' she decided, after some thought. 'And I daresay Lady Warrender will be there, with her special talent for smoothing over any awkwardness.'

Lady Warrender, however, was not there when Caroline was once more shown into the now familiar studio. Sir Oscar was there alone, sitting at his desk, and although he rose when she came in, his greeting was brief, and he merely indicated the chair directly opposite him before resuming his own seat.

There was a slight silence, and Caroline realised it was being left to her to open the proceedings.

'I hope,' she said diffidently, 'you weren't annoyed by my writing to you.'

'On the contrary,' was the reply, 'if you had not made some approach to me on your own account I should have lost interest in you and any possible career of yours.'

'Would you really?' She opened her eyes wide. 'But why, Sir Oscar?'

'Because the profession you hope to enter is a very tough one, and the prizes don't go to those who hang back expecting someone else to take the initiative for them.'

'I—I very nearly didn't write that letter,' she suddenly confided in him.

'I know.' He smiled slightly.

'*How* do you know?'

'Because everything about you the other evening indicated a retiring disposition. The only time you plucked up courage to act with boldness was when you were thinking of your cousin's welfare. Isn't that correct?'

Caroline nodded, but she added quickly, 'I'm deeply concerned still with Jeremy's career.'

'Of course, of course,' agreed the conductor without any interest at all. 'Now tell me about yourself. All I know so far is that you have obviously had a good basic vocal training, and that your voice is an excellent one, with a memorable quality essential if one is ever to stand out from the clutch of worthy Marys and Annes and Elizabeths, who never make a nasty sound nor, unfortunately, give one the slightest reason to want to hear them again.'

'Oh——' Caroline slowly digested this. 'I don't know that there's much else to tell you about me.'

'Of course there is—don't be silly,' said Warrender impatiently. 'And above all don't underestimate yourself. If you can't display the goods in your own shop window no one else is going to do it for you. Why should they? Think carefully for three minutes, and then tell me anything about yourself which you think might interest me.'

'Anything?'

'Anything,' agreed the conductor. 'The singer, unlike every other musical performer, is his or her own instrument. If the basic voice is good, everything else about the owner of it contributes to—or detracts from—its beauty and importance. Three minutes——' and he suddenly smiled at her with quite compelling charm and authority.

Afterwards Caroline had the extraordinary impression that she practically told Oscar

Warrender her life story. If it proved longer than he had expected he showed no sign of impatience. He asked one or two questions, but in a casual way which did nothing to check the flow of her narrative and usually related to her feelings or reactions.

She even told him about the concert on the previous evening, and he enquired idly, 'Did you admire Lucille Duparc?'

'As an artist—yes. As a person, I think—no.'

'How about your cousin?' he asked, moving one or two things on his desk absently, so that she thought again that he was not really much interested in Jeremy.

'He—admires her very much, both artistically and personally,' she replied, and for the first time there was hesitation in her flow of information.

'Do you mind very much?' He looked up and straight at her.

'*Passionately!*' Suddenly her remarkable eyes blazed at him, and the one word came out with a force which shook her to the core.

'Splendid,' said Oscar Warrender, and *his* one word, though quietly spoken, was as significant as hers.

'What do you mean? It—makes me very unhappy.' She glanced down at her tightly clasped hands.

'That is immaterial,' he told her coolly. 'Success—particularly artistic success—is not built on unadulterated happiness.'

'But——' indignation rose in her at this casual dismissal of her misery about Jeremy and, to her own dismay, she heard herself challenge him with, 'Have *you* ever known what it is to be terribly unhappy?'

'Of course. No fully developed person goes through life without experiencing the extremes of emotion,' he told her not unkindly. 'But your unhappiness is not the factor which made me express satisfaction. It was the way you looked and the tone of your voice. In one word and with one direct glance you showed me that you can express tremendous depth of feeling in your face and your voice. If it's any consolation to you, Lucille Duparc has to work much harder to produce an equal effect,' he added with a slight smile.

'Does she?' Caroline caught her breath. 'Do you mean that one day I might possibly be as—as arresting as she is?'

'Difficult to tell. She is the product of much work on her own part and the part of those who have schooled her. We still have to find out how you respond. The vocal foundation has been well laid by your Miss—Curtis, isn't it?—and you say you play the piano reasonably well?'

Caroline nodded.

'I would suggest that you continue your basic singing lessons with her, but in addition you will need intensive coaching in the study and interpretation of roles, the understanding of musical nuances, the value of tone colour and so on—everything which belongs to the development of an artist as distinct from a mere warbler. Apart from that——'

'Sir Oscar,' interrupted Caroline rather anxiously, 'all this is going to be very expensive, isn't it?'

'Oh, yes. The training of a worthwhile singer is not a cheap proposition,' he agreed. 'I'm only

outlining what ideally you should do. How—or
even if—you follow that out is of course your
own concern, though I can recommend you to the
right people for the purpose. In addition, if you
set your sights on an operatic career—which I
would say is your right milieu both vocally and
personally—there would be the further matter of
some stage training.'

She was silent in dismay at the immensity of
the task confronting her, and finally she said
slowly,

'I'm afraid we're talking rather far outside the
sphere of practical possibilities. As I told you, I
have a well paid but not spectacular office job. In
addition I have a modest bank balance made up
of the last of the money left me by my parents
and part of the very generous reward Lady
Warrender gave me for finding her ring. It would
be idle for me to pretend there's anyone else to
whom I could turn.'

'Think it over,' he replied calmly. 'It's
remarkable the paths one can explore if one is
utterly dedicated to a fixed purpose. What about
Kennedy Marshall? Might he feel like making a
generous contribution?'

'My employer?' Caroline sounded so shocked
that Oscar Warrender laughed. 'I couldn't *think*
of asking him for anything!'

'No?' He continued to look amused and even a
trifle curious. 'Is he the kind who would expect
something in return?'

'Certainly not!'

'I see. Well, it will be for you to consider the
situation, decide what you might undertake in the
immediate future, and canvass every possibility

for financing your programme. I think I should tell you that in my view you're probably worth a good deal of effort—and sacrifice.'

'Thank you,' she said earnestly.

'Don't thank me, thank your Maker,' Warrender told her drily. 'He gave you the voice. It's up to you to develop it.' Then, as she got up to go, he added, 'I'm not usually in favour of contests or competitions—they tend to be a gamble, and not a particularly healthy one. But there's no denying that a useful money prize would help. We'll consider that later.'

Then he dismissed her, courteously but firmly.

Caroline made her way home divided between extravagant hopes and a sense of realism which verged on despair. And once she reached home, of course, there would be no one with whom she could discuss those hopes and fears. To Jeremy—and still more to Aunt Hilda—this sudden obsession about her own vocal future would be inexplicable, even carrying a hint of treachery with it.

After all, it was she herself who had always insisted on putting Jeremy's fortunes before anything else. She it was who had agreed that her part was to wait until *he* was established. Was it perhaps, she thought uneasily, still her natural role—to wait?

But when she reflected on Sir Oscar's bracing advice—and the way Lucille Duparc had looked at Jeremy, which of course had nothing to do with the present situation—she thirsted for action. And action on her own behalf, for the first time in her life.

One encouraging ray of light was provided by

the fact that the next day was Saturday, when she would be going to her usual singing lesson. To Miss Curtis she could confide her whole story, secure in her complete interest and a discretion upon which one could rely implicitly.

As it turned out Miss Curtis was not only enthralled and prepared to be discretion itself, but she displayed an optimism beyond anything Caroline had herself entertained.

'You have a great future in front of you, dear child, if you follow Sir Oscar's advice,' she stated dramatically. 'Who else could advise you better?'

'But the money——' began Caroline.

'The *money*!' With a telling gesture of scorn Miss Curtis pushed imaginary stacks of banknotes from her. 'The money must somehow be found. To begin with, you will no longer pay for any lessons of mine——'

'Of course I shall!' Caroline interrupted indignantly in her turn. 'In fact, I fully intend to increase the very modest amount I pay you, out of Lady Warrender's generous reward. You see——'

This competition in generous offer and counter-offer continued for a few minutes and ended in their kissing each other emotionally—which was quite unlike them really—and in Miss Curtis declaring that when Caroline was famous, and she herself was known to be the teacher of the rising star, prospective students would be eagerly beating a pathway to her studio door.

Caroline's own hopes fell somewhat short of this, but there was no denying that there was something so infectious about Miss Curtis's enthusiasm that, for the first time, she began somehow to believe in miracles.

If only she could have discussed it all with Jeremy! Until a couple of weeks ago that would have been the natural, the most exciting and heartwarming thing to do. But not now. For Jeremy was, not unnaturally, pursuing his own interests with concentrated energy and enthusiasm.

Initially encouragement had been based on Sir Oscar's moderate but basically favourable verdict. But to this had now been added some subtle influence from Lucille Duparc, with whom he was quite obviously maintaining some continued contact. Indeed, during the following week the French soprano was his chief topic of conversation.

He questioned Caroline closely about Lucille's future plans. For, as he said, 'Since your boss represents her you must know quite a lot about these.'

'Plans for next year, you mean?'

'Any plans of hers.' Jeremy made a gesture descriptive of unlimited activities.

'A lot of what goes on in the office is confidential,' Caroline said a trifle repressively.

'Oh, come on! Don't be silly. I'm not asking about fees or conditions of contract or that sort of thing. But there must be a point when general trends are discussed. There's nothing specially confidential about that. Any persistent journalist can ferret out something like that.'

'Persistent journalists also exercise their lively imaginations,' retorted Caroline tartly. 'But, without breaking any confidences, I can tell you that Lucille is expected to come to the Garden in the spring to sing two—or possibly three—works, but I don't think it's been decided yet just which ones they'll be.'

'Is she, by Jove!' Jeremy was clearly enchanted with this scrap of information. 'She wouldn't tell me much about her future arrangements—she said it was unlucky to do so before everything was fixed. She's a bit superstitious, you know,' he added with an indulgent laugh which showed how charming he found Lucille's superstitions.

'You sound as though you've been seeing quite a lot of her.' Caroline tried to make that sound casual.

'Oh, on and off.' Jeremy brushed that off lightly. 'I know about the Birmingham concert at the end of the month, of course. In fact I'm going to it.'

'To Birmingham? Are you really, Jerry?' Suddenly Caroline felt deeply disturbed, and she went on with less than her usual tact, 'Does she— mind your following her around like that?'

'What do you mean—*following her around*? Birmingham isn't exactly outer space,' he retorted indignantly.

'No, no—of course not, but——'

'We get on remarkably well, to tell the truth,' he stated emphatically, cutting across her objection. 'So naturally I want to hear her as often as I can. You don't get a chance to experience *her* standard of performance every day.'

Caroline thought of that appealing photograph on the front of the programme, and Mrs Van Kroll's caustic comment on it, and her tone was troubled as she said,

'Well—so long as she isn't just stringing you along, I suppose it's all right.'

'Caroline, what's the matter with you?— making these catty comments and suggestions!' Jeremy exclaimed indignantly. 'You can take it from me that Lucille Duparc is a very special and lovely person. Incidentally, she's a very good friend too. As a matter of fact, she's trying to help me with my career. While I'm in Birmingham she's going to introduce me to someone who might get me some work on the French provincial circuit.'

'But Jerry, French agents don't go to Birmingham to make their arrangements,' countered Caroline unhappily. 'They——'

'Don't be silly,' he interrupted loftily. 'You needn't think you're the only one to know about these things, just because you work for that unpleasant Kennedy Marshall. This man isn't coming to Birmingham just to meet *me*. He's coming over to see Lucille about some of her arrangements, and she's promised to put in a word for me.'

'I see,' said Caroline pacifically, for this was obviously not the moment to say that in her experience contracts seldom stemmed from a word being 'put in' by another artist, however distinguished.

The last thing she wanted to do was to quarrel with Jeremy about Lucille Duparc. So she held her peace; but this conversation was very much in her mind the next afternoon when she was taking dictation from her employer. She glanced at his rather hard, good-looking face and could not help wondering what *his* reaction would have been to the naïve arrangements suggested for contract-making via Lucille Duparc.

She could not of course ask him; they were not on terms when they discussed anything personal. And then, oddly enough, it was he who suddenly volunteered a completely personal remark.

'I understand you went to consult our mutual friend Oscar Warrender the other evening,' he said. 'About your chances of making a career in the world of singing.'

There was nothing in his tone to indicate his own reaction to that, but hers was immediately defensive.

'Who told you?' she asked quickly.

'He did, of course. But he was rather cagey about what advice he gave you. Said I must ask you if I wanted to know.'

'And *so* you want to know?' Caroline gave a nervous little laugh. 'I didn't imagine it would be of any interest to you.'

'No? Well, I think I might be kept in the picture,' he countered. 'After all, if you're going to take off into the higher spheres of the operatic world, let's say, I shall have to start looking for another secretary. I should also expect you to remember me kindly if you required a good agent.'

At that she laughed uninhibitedly.

'No hurry,' she assured him. 'Although Sir Oscar spoke encouragingly about my future potential, he frankly outlined a programme of study which would cost far more than I could think of raising at the moment.'

'Did you tell him that?'

'Of course. There'd be no point in ignoring the practical facts.'

'And what did he say to that?' enquired her employer curiously.

'After having been kind enough to say——'

'Oscar Warrender isn't kind. What he says he means.'

'Well then, he said that in his view it would be worth a good deal of effort and sacrifice to develop the voice God had given me. And his concluding advice was for me to canvas every possibility for financing the programme he'd laid down.'

'He didn't offer to help in any way?'

'No. Why should he?'

'I don't know.' Kennedy Marshall rather moodily pushed the point of his pen into the blotting pad on his desk. Then he shrugged and said, not very agreeably, 'Well—so long as you don't expect *me* to do it.'

'You're the last person to whom I would apply,' she replied icily. 'I think I told him that,' she added for good measure.

'Very friendly of you, I must say,' he commented, and he reached for the telephone which rang at that moment.

Caroline stared out of the window with studied indifference until she heard him say, 'Who?— Yes, she's here now.' Then he handed the receiver to her. 'It's for you.'

'Shall I take it in my own office?'

'No, take it here—and make it snappy. We've wasted enough time already.'

With this encouragement, she said huskily, 'This is Miss Bagshot speaking,' and to her utter amazement the voice which replied was that of Miss Curtis.

'Don't say too much, dear! Are you alone?' the voice asked, exactly like someone in a spy thriller.

'No,' replied Caroline with commendable brevity.

'Listen, dear. I know you don't like personal calls in your office, but this is *important*. I had to tell you right away. I have a backer for you! Don't say anything—don't say anything,' the voice implored before Caroline could even draw breath to gasp. 'It's Sophie Lander—Sophie Van Kroll, you know. She's here with me now and she's prepared to pay for everything. Can you call in here on your way home?'

'Yes,' said Caroline. And then, still in the best tradition of all good thrillers, the line went dead.

CHAPTER FOUR

MECHANICALLY Caroline replaced the receiver.

'Good news or bad?' Kennedy Marshall enquired with unusual curiosity.

'Does it have to be either?'

'Well, you've just lost all your colour,' he told her. 'That suggests some kind of shock.'

'It wasn't bad news,' she said, resisting the impulse to add that he might, however, be looking for that new secretary somewhat sooner than he had expected.

She managed to control her agitation while he continued to dictate. But when he finally dismissed her with instructions to type only the last two letters and leave the others until the morning, she found she could hardly stand up. Her knees were shaking as she crossed the corridor to her own room and, for some unexplained reason, the shadow of that new secretary seemed to accompany her—an unwelcome figure.

The thought of any new secretary inhabiting *her* office, typing on *her* machine, taking dictation from *her* employer—particularly the last—was wholly unacceptable.

'Don't be ridiculous,' she told herself impatiently. 'You ought to *like* the idea of someone else coping with his moods and demands, while you're free to do the thing you've always most wanted to do. Anyway, perhaps Miss Curtis has got it all wrong and none of this is really going to happen.'

For on more mature reflection it seemed beyond the bounds of credibility that this extraordinary offer could be part of real life— even if based on the whim of a wealthy, slightly capricious woman like Mrs Van Kroll. Yet, Caroline remembered suddenly, her employer *had* informed her that she had 'made quite a hit' with his godmother.

'He won't like her doing this,' Caroline bit her lip at this thought. 'He'll think I went cadging to her on the strength of that one meeting. Unless, of course, he's not to be told a word about it.' Indeed, the way Miss Curtis had demanded top secrecy over the office telephone suggested that it was above all Kennedy Marshall who was to be kept in ignorance of the proposed arrangement.

It was useless, she decided, to speculate further on so few facts. She must wait until she saw Miss Curtis in person. Meanwhile the two letters required by her employer must no longer be neglected, for she was still no more than a secretary—not yet a rising star in the operatic firmament.

Caroline completed the task with only half her attention on what she was doing, and took the letters in for signature. Uncharacteristically, Kennedy Marshall was sitting at his desk doing nothing, just gazing thoughtfully out of the window and smiling slightly, as though reflecting on something which pleased him.

He glanced through the first letter and signed it without comment. Over the second one he frowned and asked, 'What's that?' pointing to a couple of lines near the top of the page.

Caroline looked over his shoulder and gasped slightly.

'I'm terribly sorry! I'm afraid it's my idiotic mistake. I can't think how——'

'Do it again,' he told her briefly. 'And then you'd better get off home. That pleasant shock via the telephone seems to have put you off your stroke. What was it, by the way? Some chap wanting to marry you?'

'No, of *course* not!'

'Why "of course not"? You're a very attractive girl so long as you keep that temper in check.'

'What temper? I haven't got a temper!'

'Indeed you have. You've scared the daylights out of me once or twice recently.' And he tipped back his chair and grinned up at her.

'I've told you before—the shoe is on the other foot. It's I who am sometimes afraid of you,' she said softly.

'You need not be, you know.' He brought his chair into an upright position again, removed his amused glance from her and began to write.

As she stood there beside him she had a sudden and intense longing to tell him about Mrs Van Kroll's offer and to implore him not to think she had angled for it. Then, as he took no more notice of her, she went away instead, to retype the offending letter.

This time he signed it without comment. Then he said, 'Good night,' with an air of final dismissal, evidently assuming that she would act on his advice to go home somewhat earlier than usual.

Caroline accepted the hint and went. For she now felt unable to wait any longer before receiving a full explanation of the dramatic telephone call. Indeed, in an access of anxious curiosity, she took a taxi and arrived at Miss Curtis's small house in the less fashionable part of Chelsea to find a very handsome car standing outside. Evidently Mrs Van Kroll had not yet departed.

Even before Caroline could knock with the shining brass knocker the front door was opened by a flushed and triumphant Miss Curtis, who exclaimed, 'Oh, my dear, I'm so glad you came right away!' And, ignoring Caroline's whispered, 'What's *happened*?' she ushered her into the familiar room where Caroline was used to having her singing lessons.

Mrs Van Kroll was seated in an armchair which, until that moment, had always appeared quite ordinary to Caroline. Now it seemed to have taken on a certain distinction simply because of the woman who was sitting there, and immediately Caroline recalled again the words in which Miss Curtis had described her: 'She wasn't really a good actress. She didn't need to be. When she came on to the stage or into a room you didn't notice anyone else.'

'Come here and let me look at you more carefully than I did the other evening,' was Mrs Van Kroll's greeting to Caroline, and she held out her hand with a faintly regal gesture.

Smilingly Caroline took the hand, and was aware of an intense scrutiny before Mrs Van Kroll continued, 'Yes—I see what Oscar Warrender meant.'

'Oscar Warrender!' Caroline was astounded.

'But—but I didn't know you knew him,' she exclaimed in some confusion.

'Why should you?' replied the older woman reasonably. 'Though, as a matter of fact, I know—slightly or intimately—most people of any importance in the world of music and theatre,' she added, with a matter-of-fact air which robbed the words of any offensive conceit.

'But, Mrs Van Kroll—please don't mind my asking questions—I'm so bewildered, so thrilled that you and he should have any occasion to speak of me. I'm not exactly a topic of outstanding interest.'

'You're going to be, dear,' interjected Miss Curtis.

'Is it possible that—Mr Marshall spoke about me to you, or to Sir Oscar?' Caroline found suddenly that she would very much like that to have been the case, but Mrs Van Kroll dashed the idle hope immediately.

'Dear child, I'm very fond of Ken, but I don't discuss everything with him.' She smiled, and a slight shrug dismissed him from the conversation, which Caroline faintly resented on his behalf. 'The simple fact is that Naomi here——' she smiled across at Miss Curtis'—told me about your talents, your hopes—and your difficulties. Obviously before I considered helping you I had to have an authoritative opinion about you. I consulted Oscar.'

'And he—reported favourably?' A smile of pure happiness irradiated Caroline's features.

'On your talents—yes. On your chances of ever being able to develop them he was pessimistic. I asked if it were merely a question of money——'

Mrs Van Kroll spoke with the simplicity of one to whom money never presented a major problem'—and he said that, while no one could ever guarantee the full development of someone's potential, the only way of finding out in your case would require the expenditure of a considerable amount of money. If that could be done he thought we might discover something quite unusual.'

She paused, but Caroline could find neither breath nor words to comment on this dazzling situation.

'I am, as you possibly know,' Mrs Van Kroll added carelessly, 'a wealthy woman. I am prepared to gamble on you.'

'Say something, dear,' prompted Miss Curtis in an anxious whisper, and, with totally natural grace and instinct, Caroline went and knelt beside the older woman's chair.

'There are no words in which to thank you,' she said gently. 'I can only tell you that I will work with all my heart and soul to deserve your generosity.'

'Well, that's splendid,' commented Mrs Van Kroll briskly, though she touched Caroline's cheek lightly, and Miss Curtis blew her nose quite loudly.

'How much is all this a secret?' asked Caroline then, recalling her teacher's caution as she broke the news over the office telephone. 'I mean—may I discuss it with Mr Marshall, for instance?'

'No.' Mr Marshall's godmother was quite emphatic about that. 'There's no need to seek his approval or disapproval. This is between you and me, at any rate for the six months during which we try the experiment of intensive training. If

I've made a mistake and you prove unable to benefit from the opportunity,' she explained dispassionately, 'I should prefer not to give either Ken or anyone else the opportunity of calling me a quixotic fool. Of course you will have to give some explanation for your leaving the office——'

'Leaving the office!' Caroline was dismayed to feel the way her heart plummeted at the prospect. 'Entirely, you mean? But perhaps I could make some arrangement about part-time working.'

'Perhaps.' Her proposed patron shrugged. 'You would have to be advised by Sir Oscar. He's willing to oversee your plan of work and your progress.'

'*Is* he?' Again Caroline felt she was inhabiting the world of makebelieve. 'Then what would you like me to tell Mr Marshall?'

'As much of the story as you like—but *not* that I'm financially concerned in it. I should prefer you simply to say that a friend of Naomi's has come forward with an offer of help during the experimental six months. That's true—and it's always a good idea to tell the truth if possible,' she added with an air of candour.

Caroline smiled, but said, 'I'm afraid he'll ask a lot of questions.'

'Then you must give him evasive answers, my dear,' was the unequivocal reply. 'Surely you can manage him well enough for that?'

Caroline thought of saying she could not really manage him at all, but feared that Mrs Van Kroll would find that a very spineless reply—which perhaps it would be. So she just nodded as though she felt perfectly capable of handling the situation.

'And at the end of the six months,' began Miss Curtis, who was standing by, patently eager to join in the discussion.

'Oh, yes——' Mrs Van Kroll took over again, by virtue of her undoubted right as prime mover in the campaign'—At the end of the six months, if you've made the progress Sir Oscar anticipates, we shall put you in for the annual TV contest organised by the Carruthers Trust—of which I'm a member, incidentally, although naturally I have no influence on the choice of winners.'

'But I think,' Caroline said anxiously, 'that Sir Oscar doesn't really approve of that sort of contest.'

'He will approve if you win,' retorted Mrs Van Kroll unanswerably. 'The prize money is substantial, which would help with your further studies, and you might have valuable exposure on television. Anyway, we're looking too far ahead to make decisions yet.'

She rose to her feet and proceeded to draw on her long gloves, while Miss Curtis, hovering anxiously in the middle distance, said, 'The first thing for you to do is to see Sir Oscar and hear what timetable he proposes to draw up for you.'

'Yes, of course,' Mrs Van Kroll nodded. 'And you will need to make arrangements with your office as soon as possible.'

'I hope Mr Marshall will be willing for me to stay on part time,' said Caroline.

'Would you really like to do that?' Mrs Van Kroll glanced at her with frank curiosity. 'Are you so devoted to him?'

'Oh, "devoted" isn't quite the word!' Caroline laughed deprecatingly. 'I like and respect him and——' she paused.

'Yes?—and what else?' enquired his godmother.

'Well—that's all, I think.'

'It doesn't sound much to set against the chance of a lifetime,' said Mrs Van Kroll disparagingly. And Caroline fearing she might have sounded as though she were underestimating this magnificent offer, hastened to say that of course the great training scheme ranked above everything else.

Then Mrs Van Kroll took her leave, and Caroline and Miss Curtis were left to exult over the extraordinary change which had taken place in Caroline's fortunes.

Naturally the first thing was to thank Miss Curtis repeatedly for her bold initiative in approaching her distinguished old friend in the first place. But she brushed all thanks aside, declaring (with rather excessive modesty, Caroline thought) that she had just 'had a moment of inspiration', recognised the idea as a good one and acted on it.

Since she seemed almost embarrassed by further expressions of gratitude, Caroline desisted, and, taking affectionate leave of her teacher, she at last headed for home—and any explanations she could or should make to Aunt Hilda and Jeremy.

It was not easy.

'But why *should* anyone do such a thing?' Aunt Hilda repeated half a dozen times. 'Someone unknown to you at that.'

'I had met her once,' Caroline murmured. 'And it seems she knows Oscar Warrender and they somehow got talking about me and he said I was promising.'

'Oh, Caroline, there must be some mistake! Surely he said it was *Jeremy* who was promising!'

'No, Mother——' Jeremy intervened here, and generously. 'Warrender was certainly impressed by Caroline too. As for this friend of Miss Curtis—what did you say her name was, Carrie?'

'I didn't,' said Caroline. 'She prefers to remain anonymous, though I know that sounds improbable,' she added desperately.

'It sounds a load of nonsense to me,' stated Aunt Hilda. 'Are you sure you're not making all this up, Caroline?'

'Oh, Auntie, why should I? It's all perfectly genuine, and needs to be taken seriously since it involves leaving my job, or at least——'

'*Leaving your job?*' Aunt Hilda was scandalised and a little frightened. 'And what are you to live on without a salary, I should like to know?'

'I'll pay my living expenses out of my own bank balance,' Caroline said with some dignity. 'I should hardly expect my—my patron to do that. Or I may be able to stay part-time at the office. It depends on what Mr Marshall thinks.'

'I imagine he'll think you've taken leave of your senses,' Aunt Hilda stated gloomily.

But Jeremy, with something of the affectionate support which he and Caroline had extended to each other over the years, came to her rescue once more.

'Now, Mother, why not rejoice a little on Carrie's behalf? I know this does all sound rather improbably wonderful, but wonderful things do sometimes happen in this wicked old world. As a matter of fact, I'm hoping that something marvellous is going to happen to me, but I don't want to exult too soon,' he added in parenthesis.

Then before Caroline could say any more than, 'Oh, Jerry, do you mean that——?' he went on,

'I'm truly glad for you, dear. You deserve some good fortune. Only—if you'll take a bit of cousinly advice—get that harsh boss of yours to keep your job open for you if he will, just in case you don't startle the world as a singer. Miracles do happen—but not often, as well I know. Don't take your hand off that typewriter until your first operatic contract is signed, so to speak.'

'Oh, I won't, I won't,' Caroline assured him, warmed to the heart by his sympathetic support, which she had found so sadly lacking during the past weeks.

'Well, that's the first piece of sense I've heard this evening,' commented Aunt Hilda, and, metaphorically washing her hands of her niece's nonsensical plans, she turned to her son and asked, 'What train are you catching to Birmingham tomorrow?'

'Oh, of course! You're going to the Birmingham concert, aren't you?' Caroline exclaimed. 'I hope Lucille sings marvellously and that you enjoy every minute!'

'She will—and I shall,' Jeremy assured her, and he gave her hand a hard squeeze, as though to tell her they were back on the old confidential terms once more. Consequently, when Aunt Hilda retired to bed later, and they were left alone together, Caroline found it perfectly easy to say to him,

'Jerry, you don't feel I've been a bit mean to steal a march on you, so to speak, when we've always regarded you as the only singer in the family until you get firmly established?'

'I know what you mean.' He threw a careless arm round her. 'But you've as much right as I have to try to be a professional singer. You have a long way to go, of course, and you mustn't be shattered if you don't eventually make it. Very few people do, you know.'

'I know—and thank you for being so generous and understanding.' She smiled up at him gratefully.

'Well——' he laughed musingly'—I suppose I might have felt differently if I hadn't got some fresh hopes myself instead of struggling on unnoticed and unsuccessful. But now I've got Lucille behind me——'

'Oh, Jerry, to what extent?'

'All the way,' he replied in a sudden burst of happy candour. 'We more than like each other, Carrie. We're in love—and you're the first person I've told.'

She managed somehow to say how happy she was for him and that yes, of course she would keep it a secret, and yes, of course she realised that now he must strive harder than ever to attain a position worthy of Lucille. An ambition which he seemed to regard as no longer beyond any reasonable reach, now that he had her co-operation.

Somehow Caroline managed to shut off full comprehension of what all this would mean for her. It was no longer a question of subduing anguished jealousy. It was more a fight with leaden despair, which she must conceal from him at all costs. And the only way to do that, even momentarily, was to think of him rather than herself.

That too was almost beyond natural capability, for she could not share his euphoric trust in Lucille. She was shaken by the thought that he might be indulging in groundless hopes, both professionally and personally.

Not for the first time, Mrs Van Kroll's words returned to her, and nothing in that lady's cynical view held comfort for anyone who loved Jeremy. It was possible of course that her judgment of the French singer was biased; that in fact Lucille was capable of a sincere love, which she had bestowed on Jeremy. It was easy enough to love him, as Caroline well knew. But none of her own personal glimpses of Lucille held much reassurance for her.

'Don't you agree?' asked Jeremy at that point, and she realised that her attention had wandered dangerously from her cousin's blissful rambling.

'Oh, I'm sorry, Jerry dear! It's all so exciting that I can hardly keep my thoughts on one aspect.'

She even managed to laugh quite convincingly, and he seemed to find nothing odd about her lapse of attention.

'I know what you mean. I'm in a bit of a daze myself,' he conceded cheerfully. 'It doesn't seem possible that you and I have been going on for years at a rather boring dead level——' thus did he describe the happy relationship of the past'—— I'd almost given up hope of anything exciting coming my way. Then suddenly you find a diamond ring, use it to bring pressure on a celebrated couple in the very world I'm trying to enter, and we secure their qualified support. After that—as though all this isn't enough—I meet darling Lucille and we fall in love. It's like a piece of fiction, isn't it?'

Caroline said that it was. She even brought up the well-worn bit about truth being stranger than fiction, and they laughed over that together as though it were something quite original.

But when she finally tore herself away from Jeremy's happy reflections, which he seemed prepared to continue indefinitely, she shut herself in her own room, sat on the side of the bed and stared bleakly into space.

On what was she to fix her hopes?

That Jeremy would indeed find happiness with Lucille, while she, who had loved him for years— she knew that now—must stand aside and console herself with some problematical career? Or was she to hope that her assessment of Lucille was correct, and that one day a disillusioned Jeremy just might turn to herself for consolation?

Neither prospect seemed to offer much happiness in the immediate future—or even the long-term future, come to that. The CAREER, in dazzling capital letters, which had seemed to shine like a beacon only a few hours ago, had now shrunk to a doubtful candle flame, in the light of Jeremy's news. She was lucky—oh, she knew how incredibly lucky she was!—to be offered this extraordinary opportunity. She must work very, very hard to be worthy of it. But if Jeremy had told her this evening that *she* was his love, she would have given it all up.

At least—she thought she would.

She went to bed at last with none of her

questions answered. And although she fell asleep almost immediately, she woke to a weight of depression totally out of keeping with the euphoric hopes she had discussed with Miss Curtis and Mrs Van Kroll. In addition, she had now to face the task of tackling her employer on the subject of her future plans.

Caroline knew that the choice of the right moment was always an important one where Kennedy Marshall was concerned, and it was late in the afternoon before a good opportunity arose. Meanwhile she had toyed with the idea of not telling him the great news at all until she had once more managed to consult Sir Oscar about the exact programme he proposed for her. But an innate sense of fairness told her that Kennedy Marshall was entitled to know as soon as possible what she had in mind and how far it would affect his own plans.

Consequently, when he pushed aside a pile of files and said, 'Well, we can consider that settled for the time being,' she drew a deep breath and asked,

'Have you a little time to hear something I need to tell you? It's about future working plans.'

'Fire away.' He looked at her with full attention, she noticed, which was not by any means always the case when she introduced a subject outside his own choosing.

She explained to him then, in a steadier voice than she had expected to achieve, that Oscar Warrender's good opinion of her had prompted her teacher to consult an old friend about the financial difficulties inherent in any practical plan.

'And this friend——' she was growing slightly more breathless now'——has offered to finance me for six experimental months of intensive training in order to assess what my future chances might be.'

He listened to her without interruption. Then at the end he simply said, 'So you want to leave me?'

'I *don't*,' she cried distressfully. 'It's not that at all. I mean——' she stopped.

'What exactly do you mean, Caroline?' His tone was not at all provocative. Indeed, for the first time in all her recollection of him, it was almost kindly, and suddenly she found it quite easy to complete her explanation.

'I like working here—for you. I truly do, even though we cross swords occasionally. And I love the work. But this is a chance in a thousand—in ten thousand. I can hardly believe even now that it's happened to me. That was why I was so staggered by that phone call yesterday. It was from my singing teacher, Miss Curtis, to tell me she'd found someone who would back me.'

'Not a man, I trust?'

'No. Do you mean there would be objections if it were?'

'From me personally? So far as I'm entitled to have them—yes. As you know——' he gave her that wicked smile'—I'm a nasty distrustful sort of chap, and would suspect him of ulterior motives as a matter of course.'

'A friend of Miss Curtis?' Caroline smiled incredulously.

'I should be loath to regard an elderly woman teacher as a satisfactory first line of defence. But go on. You say, in the words of the old song, that you don't want to leave me but you think you ought to go. You can't have it both ways, my dear.'

He had not often called her 'my dear', and perhaps that was what emboldened her to say quite firmly, 'If I would be any real use to you as a part-time worker, I could possibly combine the two things—for the experimental six months at any rate. If Sir Oscar agreed——'

'Oh, so Warrender is in this up to the neck too, is he?'

She explained further about the famous conductor's role as principal adviser and director of her studies, and Kennedy Marshall rubbed his chin reflectively.

'Well, I don't mind admitting that I'd be very sorry to lose you, Caroline,' he said at last. 'I suppose we might get hold of a good routine worker to take care of much of the standardised stuff. It would mean quite a lot of reorganisation, of course, but I was already considering involving you in more of the outside work. Attending performances, making personal judgments—for I've noticed your natural judgment is good—and so on. In fact, to a certain extent, I suppose you would be talent-spotting. Would that interest you?'

'I would adore it!' Caroline flushed with sudden excitement. 'If you really think my judgment sufficiently good.'

'I wouldn't have suggested it otherwise,' he told her drily. 'Well, talk to Warrander and see what can be arranged. If what I've suggested is a practical possibility to combine with whatever he has in mind for you, I'm willing to go along with it.'

'Oh, *thank* you!' She smiled at him as though he had offered her the Koh-i-noor, which was perhaps what prompted him to reply provocatively,

'Until you're sufficiently experienced for us to rely on your unsupported judgment I'm afraid you'll have to put up with my company at a good many performances. Do you think you can bear that?'

'I'll try,' she retorted lightly. And then, as she thought that sounded churlish after he had been so willing to co-operate over her plans, she put out her hand and just touched his as it lay there on the desk between them.

'Thank you,' she said again, and her tone was warm and friendly.

He turned his hand and for a moment his long, strong fingers closed round hers. Then he said almost curtly, 'You're a good child,' and dismissed her with a nod.

Back in her own office Caroline looked at her hand as though something quite unusual had happened to it. She remembered reading some-where—though she could not recall where—that 'touch is the strongest and most primitive form of communication and should be used sparingly'.

'Well, I don't often hold hands with him!' she told herself with a laugh, and turned to other matters.

Half an hour later the telephone rang, and she was summarily bidden to the Warrender presence that very evening, to discuss and arrange her initial programme.

When she arrived in his studio she was not much surprised to find that there was little discussion, in the sense of querying anything he had to say. But the amount which he had already set in motion astounded her. Apparently it had been arranged that she should attend three or four times a week a well-known Opera Studio, where less than a dozen students received intensive and highly professional training.

'You'll be behind most of them in some respects,' Sir Oscar told her, 'but vocally you'll be on a respectable level of competition. Presently I shall be able to tell in which branches you are really deficient and in which you can rely to a certain extent on what you have learned in your rather sketchy development to date. In addition I shall want you here for personal study once a week, whenever I'm in this country. You understand?'

Caroline said she understood, and then broached the subject of the suggested rearrangement at her office.

'So long as both you and Marshall understand that the demands of your musical training take precedence over anything else, I have no objection. Any other question?'

'Yes. Mrs Van Kroll is in favour of my entering for a contest organised by the Carruthers Trust in six months' time. But you said you were not much in favour of public contests.'

'In general I'm not. But in your particular circumstances it might be one way of testing your weaknesses and your strengths, and it would give you an extra incentive to work hard. Mrs Van Kroll is being very generous at the moment, but even the kindest of patronage can be a tricky thing and can cease at any moment.'

'Anyway, I don't *want* to lean on her generosity any more than is strictly necessary,' Caroline explained earnestly. 'I'm not a natural sponger, Sir Oscar, and I want to be independent as soon as ever possible.'

'I'm glad to hear it.' He smiled faintly. 'So, provided you work steadily, without pinning all your hopes on the pot of gold at the end of the Carruthers rainbow, I expect I shall let you enter when the time comes.'

'Just one more thing,' she said quickly, as she saw he was preparing to dismiss her. 'You do understand, Sir Oscar, don't you, that although Mr Marshall is co-operating over the new arrangements with his office, he has *no idea* that it's his godmother—that it's Mrs Van Kroll—who's financing me. It's very important that he shouldn't know.'

'I think you may rely on my discretion,' said the conductor gravely. 'It has been tested quite often in the course of my career. Now confirm your arrangements with Marshall as speedily as you can. I want you to report at the Opera Studio on the first of next month. Good night, Miss Caroline, and prepare yourself for working under a very hard taskmaster indeed.'

'At the Opera Studio, do you mean?'

'No—here,' he replied, and waved her away.

There was no one to whom she could report these developments at home, for Jeremy was of course in Birmingham, and Aunt Hilda ostentatiously avoided any reference to what she obviously regarded as some strange temporary delusions on Caroline's part.

Conversation therefore centred on minor domestic happenings, in which Caroline could, from long practice, display a remarkable degree of interest. Reflections on her own fortunes were, as usual, reserved for the time when she was alone in her own room.

The long talk with Sir Oscar had put fresh light and colour into the whole scheme for her projected training. So much so that even the thought of Jeremy and Lucille together in Birmingham could not detract from the excitement of having such detailed plans laid down. He had not made anything sound easy, but he had somehow made everything seem possible.

She did not know that this was part of the famous Warrender technique for getting the best out of everyone he handled. She only knew that he had fixed her attention so firmly on the attainable future that it was difficult to linger too sadly over the unsatisfactory present.

Caroline was glad that he had almost agreed to her competing in the Carruthers Contest, for only thus could she see any way of eventually repaying Mrs Van Kroll for her incredible generosity.

At the office the following day Kennedy Marshall displayed as much interest as could be expected from a busy agent with three major problems on his plate—and no more. Having established the salient fact that Oscar Warrender agreed to what he had himself proposed, he said,

'Well, start combing the agencies for someone with whom you can divide the office work. I will myself attend to the other details over the weekend when I have more time. No, don't thank me. We've been through that already and have agreed that I'm a kind, understanding fellow. Now get me the Nicholas Brenner file.' Which she did.

It was later than usual when Caroline finally reached home, to find Jeremy alone and waiting for her. By great good fortune Aunt Hilda had gone in next door to have a cosy—not to say boastful—chat with her neighbour, and Jeremy began his tale at once.

'I haven't told Mother more than half of it,' he explained. 'You know what mountains she builds out of the most modest molehills. But I sang for the French agent, Pierre Carrie, and he was really impressed. He seems pretty sure he can get me some modest but useful work in provincial France, and possibly in Belgium too.'

'Oh, Jerry!' She gave him a congratulatory hug and unhesitatingly postponed any account of her own affairs during the last twenty-four hours.

'But that isn't all,' he went on exultantly. 'He strongly hinted that some time in the future Lucille and I might do some sort of joint recital tour together.'

'With Lucille Duparc! But she's an established artist. Almost an international one, in fact.'

'Yes, I know. That's why I'm so excited.'

'But—does *she* like the idea?'

'Of course she does. Though naturally I should have to get myself better known—put myself on the map, so to speak. We all agreed about that. It would be vital that I established myself to some extent in the public eye without, of course, aspiring to her standard. There's quite an art in being a successful assisting artist, Lucille says, and I see exactly what she means.'

'Ye-es,' agreed Caroline, trying not to sound too doubtful—and failing. 'When you say you would have to establish yourself to some extent in the public eye, what do you mean exactly? It isn't easy.'

'Oh, there are ways and ways, if you know the ropes,' he assured her. 'It was Lucille herself, bless her, who came up with a splendid idea. There's going to be a very big voice contest in about six months' times. Big prizes—or at any rate a very big first prize—and wide TV coverage. You wouldn't know about it, I expect, but——'

'I might. Who's promoting it?' asked Caroline, and her voice had suddenly gone thin and apprehensive as a premonitory chill crept over her.

'Something called the Carruthers Trust. Have you ever heard of it?'

'Yes,' said Caroline slowly. 'I've heard of it.' And she shivered slightly, as though someone had walked over the grave of her hopes.

CHAPTER FIVE

DURING the next few months Caroline's life changed radically. And, inevitably, Caroline changed too.

For most of her growing-up years she had lived with a keen awareness that she owed her home and most of her general wellbeing to her aunt; and as she was a naturally sensitive and appreciative girl the feeling of indebtedness was a constant factor, which sometimes weighed heavily on her spirits.

To do Aunt Hilda justice, it had never been her intention to underline the obligation, for, in her somewhat limited way, she was a kind woman. But, with a touch of perhaps understandable complacency, she was herself virtuously aware of how much Caroline owed to her, and she assumed that Caroline would naturally be aware of it too. Which Caroline was.

Had there been no one else involved in the family set-up Aunt Hilda might well have gone to the other extreme and spoiled her niece. But by the time Caroline came along the young household god was already Jeremy, and to him Caroline willingly paid affectionate homage as a matter of course. She had never sought the limelight, and neither of the two people with whom she shared her family life had ever thought of turning it on her. Her role was a supporting one, and she willingly accepted it.

Now, quite suddenly, all that was changed. Because of the extraordinary discovery of her vocal talent, and the even more extraordinary interest and generosity of Mrs Van Kroll, she was encouraged—almost commanded—to develop as a personality in her own right. It was expected of her, in fact, that in the not far distant future she would take the centre of the stage and justify the hopes of some very important people.

Even then her devotion to Jeremy might have hindered her from applying unstinted energy and enthusiasm to her own cause. But Jeremy had gone after false gods (or, to be more precise, after a false goddess) and there was now no room for Caroline in his life. At almost the same moment, Fate—with some assistance from Mrs Van Kroll—had pointed out a completely new path, and Caroline proceeded to follow it with all the single-minded determination so far unsuspected by her or anyone else.

This determination first showed itself in the energy with which she set about finding someone to take over half of her office work. She was prepared for this to be difficult, knowing how high her employer's standards were, but almost immediately good fortune and good judgment combined to bring Dinah Gale into her life. Dinah possessed no Ph.D. and only a couple of O-levels. But her basic English was excellent, her spelling impeccable, her capacity for hard work quite phenomenal, and her willingness to learn a delight to any hard-pressed employer or colleague.

'She's exactly what we need,' stated Caroline, with a confidence born of her new attitude to life.

'If you say so,' replied Kennedy Marshall. 'You're the boss now in that department.'

In fact, so rapidly did Dinah fulfil the highest expectations that within the two weeks she had been given, Caroline was able to follow Sir Oscar's instructions and report for work at the Opera Studio of his choice.

As he had predicted, she was at first quite out of her depth in certain aspects of her studies. In others—particularly with regard to the sheer beauty and management of her voice—she was ahead of most of her fellow students. Fortunately she was a quick learner and a devoted worker, so that she soon felt pretty confident that within measurable time she would be able to make good any deficiencies in her musical background.

Her private lessons with Sir Oscar at first proved to be a mixture of terror and a sort of bewildered delight. Initially she was too much in awe of him to do herself justice. But at the third lesson he said,

'When you volunteered to sing for me without any preparation you did much better than you're doing now. Why was that?'

'I was thinking only of helping Jeremy,' she replied without hesitation. 'I wasn't thinking of impressing you on my own account, and I wasn't afraid.'

'I see. Well, stop thinking of impressing me now. I am in any case very difficult to impress. Think of the composer and how best you can serve him and his work. Have you ever considered that?'

Caroline shook her head slowly, but she looked intrigued.

'That is the basis of any worthwhile perform-ance, whether by singer, player, conductor or producer. You serve the work and the composer with all your heart and soul, trying to follow in the path which he, in his genius, has laid down. It requires a mixture of intelligence, diligence—and love. Now try that again.'

So she tried it again. And when he gave a slight nod of approval she felt happy in a way she had never been happy before, vowing to herself that any career, great or small, which she managed to achieve should be based on Sir Oscar's advice.

At home there was little comment on the change in her pattern of life. So far as her aunt—or indeed Jeremy—was concerned she continued to 'go to work' at more or less the same time. And if her times of return were more erratic than had previously been the case Aunt Hilda at any rate chose to regard this as part of Caroline's 'odd new ways'.

There were aspects of this new life which Caroline longed to discuss with Jeremy, and in other days that would have been the natural thing to do. But now he was exclusively concerned with his own affairs, reserved and even a little melancholy since Lucille had returned to France. Undoubtedly he had his plans, as Caroline had hers, but, where once they would have compared them, there was an intangible barrier now which was impossible to breach.

What did provoke home comment (and that mostly from Aunt Hilda) was that Caroline now went out constantly in the evening, either to concerts or operatic performances.

'You're very lucky with free tickets these days,'

her aunt observed. 'But I suppose if there are unsold seats it looks better to have almost anyone fill them.'

'That's one element,' Caroline conceded, accepting with some effort this lowly assessment of her worth to the musical world. 'But it's partly that Mr Marshall decided he would like to try me on outside work, in order to develop my knowledge and judgment about works and performers, you know.'

Aunt Hilda didn't know, and said so.

'Do you mean to tell me he actually sends out a slip of a girl like you on your own, to make judgments and decisions that might affect his own agency?'

'I don't always go on my own. We more often go together, so that he can advise me and—well, instruct me.'

For the time Aunt Hilda contented herself with saying, 'Tch, tch,' to indicate how poorly she regarded such a state of affairs. But a few evenings later, when Jeremy came in looking more animated and excited than he had for weeks, she suddenly said,

'Did you know that when Caroline goes junketing to all those evening performances her employer goes with her, on the pretext of instructing her in some way?'

'Instructing her?' Jeremy looked both amused and taken aback. 'In what does he instruct you, for heaven's sake, Caroline? Mother makes it sound quite questionable!'

'It's nothing of the kind!' Caroline retorted hotly. 'I'm still part of the firm, and he wants me to extend my usefulness by having some experience in assessing works and performers.'

'Sounds reasonable enough, Mother.' Jeremy grinned. 'And anyway, you're going to have to be more careful what you say about one of the best agents in the business. He's just demonstrated his own good judgment by taking on your son, as a matter of fact.'

'About time too,' replied his mother grudgingly, while Caroline cried excitedly,

'Jerry, you can't mean it? At last?'

'Didn't you know anything about it?' Her cousin gave her a curious glance.

'Of course not. I'd have told you if I had.'

'I thought maybe you'd put him up to it, though he said not when I asked him. He did say someone had spoken for me. I suppose it might have been Warrender. Anyway, Marshall contacted me, saying he wanted to hear me for himself.'

'And you never told us?' His mother was reproachful.

'I couldn't, Mother. Not after so many false starts and crushed hopes. I had to have *something* positive before saying anything to you or Caroline.'

'Anyway, it doesn't matter now,' his cousin broke in eagerly. 'Tell us what happened when he did hear you.'

'He was impressed, I'd glad to say. Said he would like to represent me, and proposed to send me to audition for one or two of the smaller opera houses in Germany. Not leading roles, of course, but invaluable experience. The sort of thing Sir Oscar suggested, now I come to think of it.'

'Small roles in minor opera houses?' Aunt Hilda made a disparaging grimace. 'Then he doesn't appreciate you properly. I always said he was no good.' (She had done nothing of the sort, of course, though perhaps she had implied it.)

'Jerry, I'm so glad for you!' Caroline hugged him impulsively, with none of the inhibitions which had spoiled much of their happy relationship recently, and he responded with equal fervour.

'I have to leave for Germany at the weekend,' he went on exultantly. 'One of the places needs an immediate replacement for Arlecchino in "Pagliacci", a role I know inside out, fortunately, and also Jacquino in "Fidelio", which will need some intensive revision. Then later I'm to go and audition for two or three other places within quite a small radius—for next season. They're all small,' he insisted again. 'But it's a beginning. If I can only get my foot in——'

'And you'll have done it without that Lucille Duparc,' added his mother, with whom the French singer was out of favour for having failed to promote Jeremy's fortunes more speedily. 'She was going to do so much for you, but she didn't come up with much in the end, did she?'

'These are early days yet,' replied Jeremy stiffly. 'Anyway, she and I are pinning a lot of hopes to the Carruthers Trust Contest.'

Caroline bit her lip, and then said as casually as she could, 'You still plan to go in for that, then?'

'Why, of course! It's the biggest thing in our— in my—plans.'

'I thought perhaps this German development might cut across the dates,' she said quickly. And in her heart she knew that had been her immediate hope. For the risk that she and Jeremy might find themselves pitted against each other in the same important contest lingered at the back of her mind like a perpetual threat.

Later she wished she had seized the opportunity to make her own plans known, for the longer she left her intention undisclosed, the greater would be his indignation and shock when he learned the truth.

But it might not come to that, of course. All kinds of things might intervene, in her affairs as well as his, and perhaps the wisest thing was not to meet trouble halfway.

So she congratulated Jeremy once more, and then hurried off to the Festival Hall, where she was to join Kennedy Marshall for a Warrender concert, at which the soloist was to be the famous but ageing tenor, Lindley Harding.

He was already in the hall when she arrived and, as she slipped into her seat beside him, she said quietly but fervently, 'Thank you for helping Jeremy to his first engagement.'

'Oh, you know about that already?' He smiled slightly.

'Yes. He came home just as I was leaving. And I can't tell you how happy it's made him—and me.'

'Well, he's good. Otherwise of course I wouldn't have dreamed of putting him forward. There's little doubt about their taking him for those two roles. They're in a tight spot and won't find anyone better at a moment's notice. It should be the real break for him at last.'

'But you took quite a chance on him, not having heard him yourself until today.' She glanced at him curiously. 'Why did you do that?'

'Why do you think?' he replied.

But before Caroline could hazard any sort of guess, applause broke out as Sir Oscar made his way to the conductor's desk.

Caroline had of course heard Warrender conduct many times before, but tonight she heard and saw him from an entirely different standpoint. She thought of what he had said about 'serving the composer and the work' and realised that, commanding though his air might be when he was in charge of his orchestra, his total rapport with the music meant that he was indeed serving the composer with a lack of personal conceit rare in conductors.

'It isn't real arrogance,' she said half to herself and half to her companion as the first pause came. 'Only the authority of a man who *knows*.'

'Not bad judgment,' replied Kennedy Marshall, and laughed softly. Then he glanced down at the programme and asked, 'Have you heard Lindley Harding before?'

'No.' Caroline shook her head. 'But he was the great Otello of his time, wasn't he?'

'He was indeed. A tremendous stage artist, but equally fine in oratorio, as you'll hear tonight. I see he's singing, "Waft her, angels" from Handel's "Jephtha", and I imagine he'll be thinking of his own daughter as he sings it. She's up there in the stage box with her husband.'

Caroline glanced up at the couple who both leaned forward as Lindley Harding made his way on to the platform. Silver-haired and very erect, though no longer young, he was a striking, indefinably elegant figure as he made his entrance to the sort of applause accorded only to the cream of popular favourites.

He started the ineffably beautiful recitative with a clarity of diction which projected every word without effort to the back of the hall, and all at once, he was no longer a handsome elderly man in a faultless evening suit. He had become an almost biblical figure, and in every word, musical nuance and facial expression he was the distraught father who had vowed a sacrifice to a jealous God, and now realised that it was his own child who had to be killed.

There was not a sound from the audience, not even a suppressed cough. Everything and everyone seemed to wait on the drama of the occasion until, with a soft, almost universal sigh, they relaxed for the heartrending air in which the sorrowing father appeals to the angels to take his child gently.

Caroline was not ashamed of the tears which came into her eyes. But she was slightly taken aback to find that two of them had spilled down her cheeks. Then she realised that her employer had taken her hand and was holding it firmly, so that she felt oddly like a child who was being comforted.

'I'm sorry,' she whispered, under cover of the applause which succeeded the one long moment of stunned silence at the end of the aria.

'No need to apologise,' he replied. 'I'd have wept myself if I were the weeping type. And I wouldn't have liked you half so well if you'd kept a stiff upper lip. Do you want to go round afterwards and meet the old boy?'

'Oh, please! Do you really mean that?'

'Certainly. And the two in the stage box, if you like. He's a very fine tenor in his own right.'

'Tell me about them,' said Caroline, her eyes shining with interest. 'I noticed that she too wiped her eyes.'

'No doubt she did. Her father was the great figure in her life for years. There was a very close and emotional relationship between him and her—until the moment when a splendid young tenor rival came along to challenge his pre-eminence.'

'What happened then?' Caroline asked eagerly.

'She married him. That's the good-looking chap with her in the box now.'

'She *married* him?—her father's rival? I call that pretty mean!'

'Even if it was a love match, Caroline?' He spoke gravely, but she noticed that those keen grey eyes were twinkling with something like amusement at her reactions.

'Oh—Do you think it was?'

'I'm not in their confidence. But to the outside world I'm bound to say they show every sign of being very happy together.'

'And her father?—did he mind dreadfully, do you suppose?'

'I imagine he disliked the position very much indeed at first.' Kennedy Marshall appeared to give the problem his serious consideration. 'And she couldn't have been very happy about it either, poor girl. It's not easy, I imagine, to be torn between two highly possessive males. Tenors, at that,' he added reflectively.

She was not aware that he studied her grave and rather troubled face with an air of amused indulgence, until he said lightly, 'I don't think more tears are in order, Caroline. I understand that peace was made and that they're a very happy family group by now.'

'Are you making all this up?' She shot him a suspicious glance.

'Certainly not. All pretty well authenticated stage gossip.'

'But, Mr Marshall——'

'Do you think,' he interrupted with sudden irritation, 'that you could bring yourself to call me Ken? At least when we're out together. There's an unacceptably Victorian flavour about "Mr Marshall" at this stage of our relationship. It makes me feel a brother under the skin to Mr Rochester.'

'Oh, but Mr Rochester was a splendid hero!' she declared.

'Thank you. Your point is taken.'

'I didn't mean that disparagingly,' she declared with a laugh. 'And I'll call you Ken, if you like.' Then to her extreme annoyance she felt herself colouring, as though in keeping with the Victorian reference, and she was glad to see the leader of the orchestra returning to the platform.

In the second half of the programme Lindley Harding again sang a Handel aria, but this time a completely contrasting one, the rousing 'Sound an alarm!' from 'Judas Maccabeus'. At the end the audience rose to their feet, as though literally obeying the call to arms, and at the same time saluting the splendid old man who could still produce the kind of clarion notes hardly ever heard in the world today.

Caroline found herself on her feet too. But Ken

Marshall, more experienced in these matters perhaps, remained seated until she glanced at him indignantly and said, 'Stop playing Mr Rochester, and get on your feet and cheer!'

Looking very much amused, he rose to his feet and clapped, but he stopped short of cheering.

Then, as at last the applause died down, Caroline dropped back into her seat and said eagerly, 'You really meant it when you said you'd take me round to meet him, didn't you?'

'Yes, of course. But there's a condition attached.'

'O-oh?' She glanced at him warily.

'Will you come out to supper with me afterwards?'

She gave a relieved laugh, because something in his tone had made her think he might propose some totally unacceptable condition.

'Well, thank you. Most certainly I will—with pleasure. What made you think I would hesitate?'

'I'm never quite sure if you like me, or merely put up with me because I'm useful—and your boss.'

'What a horrible way to think of me! Particularly after what you've done for Jeremy.'

'Do we have to drag in Jeremy!' he countered with sudden impatience. And when she hastened to apologise and explain, he simply said, 'Ssh,' in an admonitory sort of growl, as the conductor returned to the platform.

By the end of the concert, however, he seemed to have recovered his good temper and, true to his promise, took Caroline round to the artists' room. And for the first time in her life Caroline found herself being introduced as a fellow artist, albeit only a budding one herself.

'A young find of Oscar Warrender's, I hear,' said Lindley Harding, with an air of courteous grandeur which would have been slightly overdone in anyone else, but was perfectly appropriate to his style and appearance.

'Why, where did you hear that?' Caroline laughed and flushed with pleasure.

'From Anthea Warrender——' then he broke off to exclaim, 'Why, Anthea my dear! I didn't know you were in the house.'

'I promised I'd come if I could possibly get away,' she reminded him, and, as she kissed him, she added, 'You don't suppose I would miss this rare chance of hearing my favourite tenor, do you?'

Then his daughter and son-in-law came in, and Caroline would have withdrawn from the group of celebrities if Anthea had not taken her hand and said,

'You have met Caroline Bagshot, haven't you? If she works hard and fulfils all our hopes, we should be hearing some interesting things of her in the future.'

'I'm only at the very beginning!' Caroline protested.

'My dear, we've all been at the very beginning once,' the old tenor said to her, with a charm that was as compelling as that of any man half his age. 'You have my best wishes.' Then he turned to his daughter and said, 'I think we should go now.' And Caroline realised suddenly that he was very tired.

She withdrew at once, with a murmur of thanks for his kind interest, and, finding Kennedy Marshall near her, she impulsively took him by the arm and said, 'Thank you. That was absolutely wonderful!'

'What was?' he asked as they made their way out of the hall.

'Everything!' declared Caroline expansively. 'But most of all, I suppose, was the first touch of supreme star quality at such close quarters.'

'Didn't you feel that after the Lucille Duparc recital, when you met her?'

'Oh—her? No,' Caroline stated firmly. 'There's something entirely different—something with real heart—in that amazing old man, even if he is a tiny bit of a poseur.'

'Well——' he laughed '—a top grade tenor, with years of fame behind him, is an almost irresistible phenomenon. Would you like to wait here while I fetch the car?'

'No, I'll come with you,' she said. And, as they made their way to the car park, she liked the way his hand closed firmly round her upper arm while they negotiated the uneven pieces of pavement which tend to make the surroundings of the Festival Hall so perilous at night.

Having collected the car, he drove them both to a small exclusive restaurant off Piccadilly, where he was obviously well known and where they were immediately conducted to a secluded corner table. Here an attentive waiter presently came to offer discreet advice on the menu, but the choice of wines, she noticed was left entirely to Ken.

Caroline looked round with interest and suddenly said, with impulsive candour, 'I've never been anywhere like this before.'

'Do you like it?' He smiled a little indulgently.

'Very much. Is this where you bring Lucille Duparc?' Catching sight of herself in the mirror opposite, she was faintly surprised to see that her smile was oddly provocative.

'I don't make a practice of bringing Lucille Duparc anywhere,' he retorted curtly. 'Suppose I tell you that I bring only my favourite people here?'

'Oh, please tell me just that!' The smile changed to a genuinely amused laugh. 'No one has ever said anything so subtly flattering to me.'

'I bring only my favourite people here,' he said deliberately. And then, before she could recover from that, he asked carelessly, 'How's the singing going?'

She tried not to go tense, but that was the last subject she would have chosen to discuss with him. She managed to say, however, that she thought everything was going pretty well.

'Warrender satisfied?'

'As far as anyone so exacting is ever satisfied. I don't think he would use the word himself, and it's better that he shouldn't, I suppose. Otherwise I might—or he certainly thinks I might—hold back the last ounce of effort required.'

'I must come and hear you some time.'

The half indifferent tone nettled her, and she replied sharply, 'That would depend on Sir Oscar's permission, of course.'

'Or the permission of the mysterious patron,' he returned.

'I—I suppose so.' They were getting terribly near dangerous ground and, try as she would to remain calm and composed, her lashes fluttered nervously and she dropped her glance, wishing desperately that she wre not sitting directly opposite him, with that clear, penetrating gaze upon her.

'Does she herself come to hear you?'

Caroline shook her head.

'You mean that even she is not admitted to the inner sanctum of the Warrender studio?'

'No,' said Caroline baldly. And then—'I wish you wouldn't question me like this. It—it isn't your business, and I don't think you're genuinely interested.'

'I'm deeply interested, Caroline! Particularly in the identity of your mysterious patron.'

There was a long silence, until he laughed and said, 'You aren't very good at dissembling, are you?'

She tried to think of some quick, clever way of parrying this inquisition, then abandoned the idea and said flatly, 'You mean you know who it is?'

'I know who it is,' he agreed. And he smiled full at her, as though pleased at his own acumen.

She swallowed nervously. Then as he obviously meant to leave the next move to her, she said in a low voice, 'I suppose you thoroughly disapprove of what Mrs Van Kroll is doing?'

'I, my dear? I wouldn't dream of disapproving of anything my godmother chooses to do. Certainly not of the way she spends her money, if that's what you mean. Why should I?'

'Both she and Miss Curtis insisted that you should be kept in the dark. For my part—I thought you would probably decide I'd presumed on a very slight acquaintance to go cadging shamelessly for support. You did say——'

She stopped, and he asked, 'What did I say?'

'When I told you about Sir Oscar's advice and—and that it would all cost a lot of money, you said, "So long as you don't expect *me* to pay." It wasn't a very nice thing to say.'

'And your reply wasn't very nice either.'

'My reply?' Her startled gaze met his across the table. 'What did I reply?'

'That I was the very last person to whom you would apply, and that you'd told Warrender as much.'

'I said *that*?' She was a good deal shocked. 'Did you mind very much?'

'As a matter of fact I did,' he said, as the waiter brought their first course.

Caroline watched in silence as the dishes were set out, and then drew breath to make sincere apologies as soon as he withdrew. But before she could say anything her companion returned to the subject of the evening's concert, asking her opinion of several points in the various items, querying some of what she said while approving of most of it.

'You're learning, Caroline,' he told her frankly. 'You have a good ear and a lively musical intelligence.' Then he went on to tell her more about Lindley Harding and his great career, giving an absorbing account of his final performance of Otello, which remained a landmark in the history of operatic performances.

Equally, the controversial question of Mrs Van Kroll's generous patronage seemed to have been banished from the evening's conversation, and Caroline was not sure whether to be relieved that this was so or disappointed not to be able to explore his reactions further.

Afterwards he insisted on driving her all the way home, although she knew he lived in the opposite direction and tried to assure him that she was quite used to going on her own.

'Not when you're out with me,' he told her.

He even stood by while she put her key in the lock of her front door. Then, just as he turned to go, she said suddenly, in a small voice—'Ken.'

He turned back immediately.

'I'm sorry I—hurt you that time.'

He did not ask her what time she meant. He knew as well as she did that they had broken off their earlier conversation at a point which left a very ragged end.

'Are you?' He looked down at her in the light from a nearby lamp. And because it was difficult to meet his eyes she just nodded, her head still bent.

'Look at me,' he said abruptly, and she looked up, startled.

To her amazement, he took her face between his hands and kissed her on the lips with unexpected gentleness. Then he laughed and said, 'You're forgiven,' before he turned away and went to his car.

She didn't stay to see him drive off. She went quickly into the house, closed the door quietly behind her and leant against it, the back of her hand to her lips, until Aunt Hilda called out, 'Is that you, Caroline?'

CHAPTER SIX

UNTIL that conversation with her employer after the Warrender concert it had not seemed specially strange that Mrs Van Kroll appeared to take little interest in the expensive training for which she was paying. But when Kennedy Marshall asked carelessly if her "mysterious patron" ever came to hear her lessons she thought, 'Why *doesn't* she at least ask Sir Oscar if she may hear me?'

She referred the question to Miss Curtis at her next singing lesson, but her teacher looked vague and said, 'Well, Caroline, I suppose she has a lot of varied interests and you are just one of them.'

'It seems an awful lot of money to spend on something which only mildly interests one,' Caroline insisted.

'But she's very wealthy, you know, and though generous, I think one must also admit that she's—capricious. Having impulsively committed herself to this enterprise, I imagine she just pays over the cheques periodically and—well, that's that.'

'Has she never discussed it further with *you*?'

'No, I can't say she has. I went to tea with her at her home about a month ago and we talked of old days—and of you, of course. She said how much she liked you and that she hoped you would be successful in your career, which I know you will be, my dear. Your progress has been phenomenal since Sir Oscar took you in hand.'

'I hope so, I hope so. But sometimes—I mean quite recently—I've begun to worry about the amount of money Mrs Van Kroll must be putting out on my behalf. Have you any idea how much it must be?'

Miss Curtis shook her head and suggested that perhaps Sir Oscar contributed his own services for nothing.

'I simply don't believe that,' replied Caroline firmly. 'Why should he? And anyway, when I first consulted him, he was quite specific about the fact that it would cost a great deal of money and that I must look round very determinedly for some way of financing what might be—not *would* be, remember, but *might* be—a fine career.'

'And we found someone, didn't we?' Miss Curtis smiled complacently. 'So what are you worrying about?'

'I know, I know. And I can never be sufficiently grateful for the way you moved on my behalf. But—don't you see?—I'm sinking deeply in debt to someone who's almost a stranger to me, and apparently has no special personal interest in me. Not even enough to want to hear me for herself.'

'She isn't a stranger to *me*, remember. We're very old friends,' stated Miss Curtis a little huffily.

'Yes, of course, dear, but——'

'I don't know why you're suddenly making all this fuss, Caroline, when everything is going so smoothly. My very rich, very generous old friend wanted to help you—perhaps primarily because you were a pupil of mine. She can afford to indulge her—whim, if you like, so why should she not do so? What's suddenly made you query the whole arrangement?'

'I had supper with Ken—with my employer—the other evening. He teased me a little about what he called "the mysterious patron" and finally admitted that he knew who it was.'

'He *knew?* But I thought—I mean, we were so careful——'

'Yes, I know. Mrs Van Kroll particularly didn't want him to know about it, did she? But I'm not very good at lying, and he got the truth out of me. And then I asked him outright if he minded his godmother spending all that money on me, and he was quite casual about it and said he wouldn't dream of objecting to anything she did with her own money.'

'He said that?' Miss Curtis rubbed the bridge of her nose thoughtfully. 'Then that's all right, isn't it? and again—what are you worrying about?'

'I suppose our conversation highlighted the fact that I was taking a lot of money from a virtual stranger, without any guarantee of ever being able to return it.'

'When you're rich and successful——'

'But suppose I never *am* rich and successful?'

'My dear, Sophie Van Kroll would never expect you to *pay back* the money! Whatever made you think of such a thing?'

'My own self-respect,' replied Caroline, setting her mouth in a firm line. 'I know that was not her idea, and I'm deeply grateful for her generous intention. If she were having marvellous fun out of her gamble perhaps I might feel differently. But to take all that money from someone I hardly know and then not be able to deliver the goods, so to speak—that sticks in my throat.'

Miss Curtis regarded her thoughtfully and then said, 'Did your employer say something the other evening which suddenly made you feel weighed down by this obligation?'

'No.' Caroline slowly shook her head. 'I might have expected him to do so, but he didn't. He was quite good-humoured about it, to tell the truth.'

'Then, if you don't mind my saying so, dear, I think you're being very silly and tormenting yourself unnecessarily. Stop worrying about it all and just work hard—and perhaps you'll win the first prize in the Carruthers Contest. Then you can make the grand gesture and offer to pay Sophie back.'

'Oh—the Carruthers Contest!' Caroline shrugged impatiently. 'I've never told you—it all seemed so complicated—but Jeremy is going in for that contest too.'

'Your cousin!' Then, as Caroline nodded, she added almost contemptuously, 'He wouldn't have a chance against you.'

'You're prejudiced.' Caroline smiled faintly. 'Or if you're not—and I really am capable of beating him—where do you suppose that leaves me? I've encouraged him and believed in him for years. I've always been on his side, you might say. He hasn't the faintest idea that I propose to go in for this wretched contest. What sort of a slap in the face do you suppose it would be if I just sailed in at the last minute and took the first prize—from Jeremy?'

'There would be other contestants,' objected Miss Curtis very reasonably, but Caroline shook her head and said,

'So far as we were concerned there would only be each other.'

There was a short silence, then Miss Curtis cleared her throat with an air of determining to do battle on all fronts.

'Caroline, people don't reach the top of a competitive profession by generously considering the feelings of a rival. Even—' she put up her hand to stop the angry interruption '—even if they are devoted to that rival. You have, as you say, accepted most generous help from Sophie. You owe it to her—to all of us—to do your best to justify that help.'

'I know! I think of it constantly,' cried Caroline distressedly. 'In fact it weighs on me so much that I sometimes think I'm beginning to lose my nerve——'

'You mustn't say that!'

'But it's *true*. If I fail, the person who stands to lose a horrible lot of money is a generous near-stranger. It would be bad enough if a friend—an intimate—someone like you, for instance, had made this tremendous gesture. Somehow I could make up for it to someone I *know*. But from a stranger—a generous stranger who hasn't even seen me to speak to since the arrangements were first made—oh, it's unbearable!' And suddenly Caroline buried her face in her hands and gave a muffled sob or two.

'You mustn't be hysterical, dear.' Miss Curtis touched the bent head in a troubled way.

'I'm *not* being hysterical,' retorted Caroline. 'I'm just miserable—and frightened.'

'If only—' Miss Curtis began, then she stopped and bit her lip. 'Caroline,' she said, with sudden resolution, 'would it really help if it were someone you knew? Like me, for instance, or—or—well, someone not a stranger? Would you feel less nervous, less anxious about your future?'

'Yes, I've said as much.' Caroline looked up, but from her expression it was obvious that she was still contemplating no more than an academic possibility.

'Then, although I gave my word—I'm going to break it.' Miss Curtis swallowed guiltily. 'If it makes you feel better, my dear, it was *not* Sophie Van Kroll who supplied the money, although she had a friendly interest in you as my pupil.'

'She—didn't?' Caroline went white and then, a dismayed look coming over her face, she cried, 'Oh, it wasn't you, was it? Oh, you couldn't—you shouldn't—It must represent half your savings. I'd never have agreed if——'

'I didn't,' stated Miss Curtis categorically. 'I just don't possess that sort of money. It was your employer who financed the whole thing. Kennedy Marshall.'

'Ken? I don't believe it!' Caroline sprang to her feet and then began to pace up and down the room, repeating, 'I don't believe it, I don't believe it——'

'But it's true.' Miss Curtis looked rather scared at the reaction she had provoked. 'Sophie agreed to be the smokescreen, as you might say. He insisted you shouldn't know where the money came from, because if you knew you would refuse to accept it. He seemed to think you disliked him—thought poorly of him, in fact——'

'How could he? Of course I don't dislike him. Nowadays I think—well, that's not the point. We scrapped at times, and he said some horrid things to me about not expecting him to pay for my training, and I said—well, that doesn't matter either, but I hate even to think of it now. The whole situation is crazy—impossible. Why have such a complicated mystery, for heaven's sake? Why wasn't he frank with me and——'

'But *would* you have taken the money if you'd known it came from him?' asked Miss Curtis obstinately.

'No, of course not! How could I? All that money from a man who was just my boss, who didn't even——'

'Well, there you are. He said it was the only way to see that you got your training and your chance.'

'He said—*that*?' Suddenly Caroline felt her lip quiver and she had to bite it hard in order to retain her composure. 'I never thought it—mattered to him,' she said half to herself. And then, as though whipping herself into fresh indignation with *some*body, 'Why all that nonsense about your phoning me at the office and pretending it was all Top Secret? And all the time there he was sitting opposite me. He made me take the call in front of him, in his office—I remember now! He was thoroughly enjoying himself, I suppose. It's maddening!'

'Don't you think he was entitled to a little fun when he was paying out all that money?' Miss Curtis sounded reproachful. 'I can tell you I enjoyed it!' And suddenly her eyes sparkled mischievously as they must have done in the days when she and Sophie Lander shared a theatre dressing room and giggled over the antics of their respective beaux.

'One doesn't like to be made a fool of,' muttered Caroline.

'Oh, Caroline, have a little generosity! Forget your own dignity and be thankful for Kennedy Marshall's generosity.'

'But that's just it!' Again she had difficulty in keeping the tremor from her voice. 'It's to *him* that I owe everything now. It's because of *his* money that I have no choice about the Carruthers Contest. I simply have to go in for it now, Jeremy or no Jeremy—*and I have to win.* I'll thank him at once, of course, and tell him——'

'You'll do nothing of the kind!' Never before had Caroline heard that tone from her friend and teacher. 'I told you all this in confidence, because you were wallowing in self-pity and sapping your artistic and moral strength about your debt to Sophie, whom you were pleased to call a virtual stranger. I did violence to my own sense of integrity by telling you the truth, hoping to console you——'

'*Console* me?' Caroline gave a mirthless little laugh.

'Yes. And I thought it was time you knew what you owed to the people who love you——'

'Kennedy Marshall doesn't love me,' Caroline said rebelliously, but she looked a little ashamed of herself. 'He was my boss and a very ruthless boss at times—why should he want to do this tremendous thing for me?'

'Caroline,' said Miss Curtis solemnly, 'the Bible says it is more blessed to give than to receive, and there are people, fortunately, who sometimes derive great pleasure from making a generous gesture. If they know that gesture will be misunderstood they are satisfied to dispense with any acknowledgment, but they make the gesture just the same. Those to whom such a gift is made are only called on to accept with grace, and not to grizzle about obligations.'

There was a long silence. Then Caroline crossed the room and kissed her teacher.

'You're perfectly right,' she said humbly. 'I accept the position as it is and will work all the harder because of it. Then if I do win the Carruthers Contest—*when* I do, I mean—I shall feel free to tell him that it was my gratitude to him which enabled me to do so.'

'Well, come, that's better,' Miss Curtis declared approvingly, and she had the tact and self-control not to add, 'And let Jeremy take his chance.'

From that moment Caroline's whole attitude towards her studies took on a new strength. She was at last someone who knew exactly where she was going.

Characteristically, it was Oscar Warrender who first noticed the change. And presently, although he was not a man to be lavish with his praise, he told her at the end of one lesson that she was making quite remarkable progress.

'If you go on like this, I shall look forward to conducting for you myself one of these days,' he said, and she thought this was not entirely in joke.

With her employer she tried to be as she had always been, but it was not easy, and she told herself with a touch of wry amusement that she was now learning to act as well as to sing. It was hard to say whether the conversation with Miss Curtis or that unexpected kiss when he bade her goodnight at her own front door recurred more often to her. But together they had generated in her a sort of shy curiosity about him which was very far from the mood in which she had once called him a mean bully.

When he was amusing and indulgent to her, as he was sometimes when they were out together, she secretly wanted to pay close attention to his reactions and to ask him why he had said this or done that. But then she would remember that he preferred to be the unknown benefactor in her life and that interested personal questions were probably not in order.

Ironically enough, Dinah Gale was able to be much franker in her assessment of him.

'He's really rather a darling, isn't he?' she said quite unemotionally one day, when neither she nor Caroline was particularly busy.

'Well, he's a good boss,' Caroline admitted moderately.

'That's what I meant. I had two bosses before him and they were both horrors.'

'Were they really?' Caroline looked interested. 'In what way?'

'Oh, the usual way, you know. One couldn't keep his hands to himself and I had to slap his face in the end. The other was just a mean bully. You couldn't say either of those things of Mr Marshall, could you?'

'Certainly not,' said Caroline, and then had the grace to blush; but fortunately Dinah's attention was distracted at that moment by the ring of the telephone.

But somehow that was what made Caroline suddenly decide to make a suggestion which was against her better judgment, but had all at once become irresistible. Immediately, as though on cue, he sent for her to take some confidential dictation.

The work took no more than a quarter of an hour and then, as he was about to dismiss her, she drew a deep breath and said, 'You asked me if Mrs Van Kroll had ever come to hear one of my sessions with Sir Oscar, and although, as I told you, she hasn't, I—I wondered if you yourself would care to come sometime? Of course if it doesn't interest you——'

'But it does.' He looked up from his work and smiled. 'I would have suggested it myself if I hadn't thought you would reject the idea out of hand.'

'I suppose at one time I might have done so. I'd have been nervous, you see, and have felt I might prove very unimpressive to anyone as knowledgeable as you. But Sir Oscar seems quite pleased with me these days, and if you promise not to expect too much, I think I would like to have your opinion.'

'When is the next session?' he asked, reaching for his desk diary and beginning to flick over the pages.

'On Thursday. But you'd have to ask Sir Oscar's permission first.'

'Of course.' He made an entry. 'I'll be there.'

'And—and don't expect too much, will you?' she said, her nervousness increasing now that she had taken the plunge.

'I'll keep a perfectly open mind,' he told her. 'And I take it you will want my candid opinion, whether good or bad?'

'Yes,' said Caroline, not very truthfully, for it had suddenly occurred to her that if he betrayed disappointment or indifference it would be her obvious duty to tell him she was aware that he was the unknown benefactor and that she could no longer accept his help for something which he felt was not worthwhile.

'It would all be over then,' she thought desolately. 'No career, no triumph. Just a return to office life. And not with Ken either. You can't remake a failed singer into a secretary. It would just be goodbye and thanks for the chance.'

And somehow that seemed the worst possibility of all.

But when she returned home, nervous and depressed, she found Aunt Hilda in excellent spirits over a joyous letter from Jeremy.

'I shall have to wait until I return to give you all the details,' he had written. 'But I can tell you right away that I'm having a genuine success! They are apparently delighted with both the roles I've done here, and when I said I was going to audition for some other houses, the Director said, "What for? Don't you like working with us?"'

'Of course I said I was only too happy to do so, and he talked about a contract for next season. Imagine that! They *want* me to continue here. Oh, the joy of being wanted instead of being regretfully rejected! Naturally, since Marshall got me the chance to audition for some other places I shall do so. It's always good to have two or three cards in one's hand. You can tell him from me, Carrie, that I'm grateful to him beyond expression.'

So she told Ken the following day, and he

nodded as though Jeremy's success did not surprise him. Then he suddenly gave her that flashing, wicked smile and asked if he might look forward to representing *her* when opera houses were competing for her services.

'Don't make jokes like that,' she said quickly. 'I'm not superstitious, but——' she crossed her fingers'—I get nervous when you talk so without having heard so much as three notes from me. You don't really know yet if I'm good—or just mediocre.'

'Warrender doesn't usually show interest in the mediocre,' was the drily humorous reply. 'But we won't actually discuss the contract until after Thursday evening if that's how you feel,' and he laughed.

'He's still not taking me seriously,' she thought, a little nettled.

But then why all that money poured out on her proposed career? The only answer was what Miss Curtis had quoted to her: 'He said it was the only way to see you had your training and your chance.'

He had wanted her to have her chance. The thought of that touched her again so deeply that her expression changed without her being aware of it, until he asked 'What's the matter?'

'The matter?' Caroline looked up, startled. 'Nothing's the matter. Why do you ask?'

'Because you looked for a moment as though you were going to cry. Does it really worry you so much that I am coming to hear you, Caroline? If it does we'll call it off.'

'Oh, no! No, of course not. I'd *like* you to hear me.' And suddenly she knew that was true, and vowed to herself that she would sing her very best for him.

This resolute mood lasted right up to the moment when they walked into Oscar Warrender's studio and he said to Ken, 'So you've really come to hear her at last? It was time.'

'What do you mean by that?' Ken asked.

'You'll see,' was the reply. 'What are you going to sing for him, Caroline?'

Until that point she had not really decided but, on sudden impulse she said, 'I'll sing the great aria from "Adriana Lecouvreur" where she tells her admirers she's only the humble handmaid of her art.'

'With any special thought in mind?' asked Ken in a rather odd tone.

'No. Why?'

'I'll tell you afterwards. Let's see what you can do with "Io son l'umile ancella".'

So Warrender turned to the piano and began to play the introduction to that lovely aria, and Caroline forgot everything but the necessity and privilege of doing full justice to it. It was ideally suited to her voice, and the months of intensive work which she had experienced with Warrender gave to her interpretation something far beyond what might be expected of a mere student.

At the end there was such a long silence that Caroline looked across anxiously at her employer. And then Warrender laughed softly and said, 'You can kiss her if you like. She's earned it.'

Ken got up, came across to her and looked down at her.

'May I?' he said, and she nodded wordlessly.

It was not much like the way he had kissed her before. For one thing he was quite unsmiling and, for another, his lips remained on hers for a fraction longer. Then Warrender said in a satisfied sort of tone, 'She's quite something, isn't she?'

'She's quite something,' Kennedy Marshall agreed. Then, as though he suddenly realised that the scene had become too intense, he laughed and said, 'May I be your agent and represent you, Miss Bagshot?'

She laughed too, though a trifle shakily, and said, 'Indeed you may, Mr Marshall.'

After that she sang several arias for him, and presently Anthea came in and asked, 'What do you think of her?'

'That I'd better sign her on as one of my artists before anyone else discovers her. When she sang the Adriana monologue, I felt like Michonnet, poor devil.'

'Why do you say that?' Caroline asked.

'Michonnet is in love with the great actress, Adriana Lecouvreur, but he's just the poor old stage-manager. As he says himself, she's so far above him that he must be satisfied just to watch her, admire her—and dream. I saw the point, poor old so-and-so. Agents are perilously near stage-managers in some respects.'

'You're perfectly absurd!' Caroline laughed outright. 'And let me reassure you that you're just not cut out by nature to take a humble back seat.'

'Too bad,' he replied with a mock sigh. 'I thought I was playing the part so well. What are your plans for Caroline, Warrender?'

'Nothing specific at the moment,' was the cautious reply. 'She's set on going in for the Carruthers Contest. At least, I think that's still your intention, isn't it, Caroline? Or have you thought better of that?'

'Oh, no, no. I *must* go in for it—and I must win the first prize,' she replied almost passionately. 'I can't continue to work and live on the generosity of—of my kind patron. It would be—dishonest to keep it up too long.'

'It wouldn't be anything of the sort, provided the patron wanted to go on helping,' growled Kennedy Marshall unexpectedly.

'I understand there's no difficulty there, Caroline,' said Warrender smoothly. 'It's just between you and her, surely.'

'It's between me and my self-respect,' replied Caroline, as she had to Miss Curtis. 'I'm going in for that contest. Why are you so much against it?'

'For one thing, it's seldom that the right person wins,' said Warrender cynically. 'And, for another, these contests are not the healthiest thing for aspiring artists—whether they win or lose. The winners inevitably see themselves as halfway to world success when they're only at the beginning, and the losers are disappointed and disillusioned out of all proportion to their relative failure.'

'But with a panel of competent judges——'

'One forceful member of the jury can sometimes sway the others,' declared Warrender carelessly.

'Oh, no!''

'Oh, yes.' Then he smiled across at his wife and added, 'I'm ashamed to say I've even done it myself. But that's years ago—and in a very good cause.'

Caroline looked shocked and disbelieving, until Anthea laughed and said, 'He first heard me as a raw beginner in a not very important contest. The other judges wanted me to win, but Oscar knew that a quick, cheap success, including exposure on quite the wrong scale, would spoil my whole development. He talked them out of it.'

'Weren't you furious?' Caroline opened her eyes wide.

'Livid,' said Anthea cheerfully. 'But I forgave him later,' she added, lightly touching her husband's arm, 'when he'd make a real artist of me.'

'But as I have my hand on you from the beginning, and intend to see that you are guided in the way you should go,' Warrender told Caroline, 'I'll indulge you over this contest. I hope, however, that whether you win or lose you will continue to accept my advice.'

'Oh, Sir Oscar, of course! What better guidance could I have?'

'None,' he said, without false modesty, and they all laughed.

This time Ken did not offer to drive her home. Instead, he called a taxi and before handing her into it he said, 'I'm totally impressed, Caroline. All joking apart, I want you for one of my artists when you're ready for public work. Is it a bargain, or do you want to think it over?'

'I don't need to think it over. And—and thank you. You don't know how happy I am.'

'I could say the same to you.' He held her hand and smiled down at her. 'As you know, I'm off to

Paris in the morning, and am not quite sure when I shall be back. I have a lot of people to see.'

'Lucille Duparc?' she enquired cheekily because she felt in riotous good spirits.

'Among others.' His reply was a little curt. 'But when I get back we'll draw up that contract. Agreed?'

'Agreed,' she said, and impulsively held her face to him.

She thought he was a trifle surprised—though why he should be when he had been only too ready to kiss her, back there in the studio, she really didn't know. In any case, he immediately bent his head, lightly kissed her cheek and then turned to pay the taxi driver, who had been looking on with obvious approval.

'Nice-looking chap, your boy-friend,' he observed chattily as they drove away.

'He's not my boy-friend,' Caroline countered quickly. 'He's my boss; quite a difficult boss at times. But this evening is special.' Somehow she had to tell someone! 'I'm hoping to be a singer, and he's just heard me for the first time and thinks I'm good. I feel terrific.'

'And so you should, a pretty girl like you,' the driver said heartily. 'Don't let any of the other girls in the chorus get their hands on him. He's the kind they all run after.'

She laughed, but she thought, 'I suppose he is! With those good looks and that vitality—and everything.'

And she was smiling so radiantly when she came into the house that Aunt Hilda said, 'Have you found another diamond ring? You look just as though you have.'

'Not quite, Aunt Hilda. But I sang for Ken—for my boss—this evening, at Sir Oscar's studio, and they were both very pleased and complimentary. It made me feel good.'

'I expect it did,' was the quite kind reply. 'But don't get a swelled head, dear. It's hard coming down to earth with a bang.'

Caroline agreed that it was, and then caught up a telegram from the mantelpiece, exclaiming, 'Is this from Jeremy?'

'Yes. I was just going to tell you. He's coming home on Wednesday, and—you'll see—he's got that contract he was hoping for.'

'Oh, Aunt Hilda! You must be proud of him. I know I am.'

Aunt Hilda said modestly that she was not counting on too much yet but that yes, she was proud of him.

Between then and Jeremy's arrival Caroline alternated between happiness on his behalf and her own, and the realisation that now she must at last admit to her proposed entry for the Carruthers Contest. Perhaps he would not feel so badly about it now that he had his foot on the ladder. But nothing, she supposed, *nothing* could sweeten the fact that she would be challenging him directly in the contest on which he and Lucille were counting so much.

'I'll just have to trust to the inspiration of the moment,' Caroline told herself, knowing perfectly well that moments of that kind provided few inspirations.

But when Jeremy finally arrived, the sheer pleasure of seeing him so happy, so sure of himself at last after all the disappointments and setbacks, swept away every other consideration. It was like old times when he hugged and kissed her as well as his mother, and said how much he had missed them both in spite of having had such a thrilling time in Germany.

'You must tell us *all* about your triumphs,' Aunt Hilda said.

To which he replied, very truly, that one did not exactly have triumphs in smallish roles, but that the opera director had been emphatic about wanting him back. In addition, he had received tentative offers from other small opera houses, which had resulted in the offer from his original house being substantially increased.

'The only snag is that I have to go back almost immediately, and I hate leaving you again so soon. But it's the best of all possible causes, so I can't complain.'

'But what about——' Caroline could hardly get out the words'—what about the Carruthers Contest, Jerry? It's coming up soon.'

'Yes, I know. But I'll just have to pass it up this year. Maybe next year. We'll see what I'm doing then.'

'You mean——' Caroline was suddenly radiant and her voice shook'—*that you're not going in for it, after all?*'

'That's what I mean.'

'Oh, Jerry, the relief! I've been feeling so awful, because I'm going in for it myself, and the thought of pitting myself against you, of all people, made me feel so mean, so disloyal. And now—you really mean it?—I can go in with a clear conscience?'

'You certainly can, you bold, bad girl.' He

ruffled her hair affectionately. 'But aren't you pitching your hopes a bit high? It's a very stiff contest, you know. Not really for amateurs at all.'

'I know,' said Caroline humbly. 'But Sir Oscar thinks I should try. At least, not quite that,' she amended, feeling she was certainly taking Sir Oscar's name in vain. 'He said I could if I really wanted to.'

'Silly girl, isn't she?' commented Aunt Hilda almost indulgently, and she actually went into the kitchen to make a personal inspection of the supper which was cooking.

'Jeremy,' Caroline said, recalling something vital, 'what does Lucille think about your cancelling? She was so keen for you to go in, wasn't she? You and she were counting such a lot on——'

'That's over.' Jeremy's expression was suddenly grim.

'What's over?' She stared at him.

'Any joint plans between me and Lucille.'

'Oh, Jerry, I'm so sorry! That is—has it spoiled things for you? You seemed so happy, so——'

'No,' Jeremy replied deliberately. 'I'm simply not going to let it spoil things, as you say. I'm on the up and up, Caroline, and no one is going to spoil that for me. Certainly not a little go-getter like Lucille. The truth is that she wanted much bigger fish than I was. I was just a bit of fun while she went after something bigger. She got him, incidentally,' he added reflectively.

'What do you mean?'

'I came through Paris on my way home and made it my business to see her and find out what she was really up to. She couldn't have been more off-brushing——'

'Oh, Jerry, I'm truly sorry.'

'Don't pity me. Pity the other chap,' Jeremy said heartily. 'I'm sorry for *him*. He deserved better than that. I know, for I've got to appreciate him after all he's done for me.'

'What are you talking about?' Caroline suddenly got to her feet, her mouth and throat so dry that she thought she would choke. 'Who— who is the man who supplanted you?'

'Well, I'm just telling you. Kennedy Marshall. She told me about it in our revealing interview and showed me the ring he'd just given her, poor dupe. Why, Carrie, what's the matter? Are you feeling faint or something?'

CHAPTER SEVEN

'Is something the matter?' asked Jeremy again. But Caroline just shook her head and then managed after a moment to force out a few words.

'No, nothing's the matter,' she said tonelessly. For not even to herself could she find any reason for the sense of utter desolation which had suddenly overwhelmed her.

'You don't like Lucille, do you?' He glanced at her curiously.

'I hardly know her.' Caroline was beginning to recover her self-possession. 'But what I know I don't like. Candidly, I'm glad to hear that you and she are no longer friendly.'

Aunt Hilda came back into the room at that moment and asked, 'Who is no longer friendly with Jeremy?'

'Lucille Duparc. She's—friendly with Kennedy Marshall instead.' Caroline hardly knew why she added that, but she managed to laugh as though she found the quick-change situation rather amusing.

'Well, he ought to be able to manage her,' said Aunt Hilda philosophically. 'He's literally been her manager for some time, hasn't he?'

'Professionally, yes.' Caroline wondered desperately how they could get off this subject. But Aunt Hilda soon came unknowingly to the rescue. Jeremy and his affairs were the only topics which could hold her interest that evening, and if Caroline contributed little to the conversation no one seemed to notice.

By a supreme effort she contrived to keep the thought of Ken and Lucille in the background of her mind. 'I'll think about it later,' she told herself. 'I'll think about it later.'

And much later, in the blessed privacy of her own room, she did exactly that, bringing from the recesses of her consciousness the stunning fact that Ken was now engaged to Lucille Duparc. That Jeremy had in the process escaped seemed oddly unimportant.

Two months ago that would in itself have been enough to make her happy beyond expression, she thought, and she wondered bewilderedly what had come over her. She loved Jeremy still and could only rejoice that he had escaped from the Lucille entanglement almost unhurt. But—Ken!

She told herself that she was disappointed in him—that she would have expected him to show more sense and judgment. But that seemed a poor reason for the sense of shock and near despair which she was experiencing. She knew now of course that he was a man of generosity and sensibility, and how could such a man be happy with Lucille?

'I should hate him to be unhappy,' she thought. 'He's been so good to me in many ways. I *like* him and——'

Then she stared across at her reflection in the mirror, as she had done on another occasion when she faced the truth about herself.

'Don't be a fool,' she said aloud. 'You love him.' And burying her face in her hands, she allowed the overwhelming truth to wash over her like a tidal wave.

That was not the end of her self-communing. Painstakingly she went back over the last few months, trying to find the moment when her relationship with him had undergone this drastic change. But, of course, like all big changes in relationships, it had been a gradual process, culminating in the shock of discovering that he was the generous patron providing the where-withal for her to follow her heart's desire and strive to become a singer.

Was that before or after the first time he kissed her? she asked herself irrelevantly. Or perhaps, she decided, it was not exactly irrelevant. For that moment was etched on her memory now with a poignancy which hurt—and it had been *before* she knew of his extraordinary generosity.

When she reached even farther back into her recollections she could not remember any time when she had found him without interest. Not when she feuded with him over Jeremy, nor when she had staggered him with the accusation that he was a mean bully to threaten her with dismissal. She remembered those scenes, not in the monotone of idle recollection, but in the brilliant colours of flashing and exciting conflict.

'I think that was the first time he really took my measure as an individual,' she reflected with a faint smile. 'That was the moment when we broke the mould of secretary and boss. And ever after that——'

She broke off suddenly in unbearable distress, for he was engaged to Lucille now and she herself was nothing in his life.

Nothing? She got up and walked softly up and down the room. Nothing?

'But I'm the girl he thinks might develop into a successful singer—a fine artist. He's backed me to do so, and I'll do it! I will, I will! I'll challenge Lucille on her own ground. *She shall not have him.*'

Caroline did not glance at herself in the mirror again. Had she done so she would have seen someone who in every line and feature commanded the stage. That the stage was no more than her own bedroom in Aunt Hilda's house was immaterial. The centre of that stage was hers by right of an iron determination and a total belief in herself.

Inevitably this mood of high courage and determination wavered in the light of day, but some of it remained, to inform Caroline's thoughts and actions—and development.

This did not go unnoticed, and later that day she overheard Aunt Hilda say to Jeremy, 'Caroline is tending to give herself airs, I'm afraid. She really thinks she *is* going to be a great singer. It's rather pathetic really, isn't it?'

'No,' was Jeremy's reply. 'It will only be pathetic if she fails. We all have to have the inner conviction that we're something special. But I wish she were not going in for the Carruthers Contest. She can have no idea of the standard required, and I'm afraid she may be in for a shock.'

'I suppose a lot of hopefuls go in for it?' Aunt Hilda sounded no more than mildly interested, but Caroline listened eagerly—and shamelessly—for Jeremy's reply.

'Well, it varies from year to year, but seldom attracts less than about eighty, I imagine. The first prize is three thousand pounds, which is not to be sneezed at, and even the lesser ones are quite useful sums. Of course a lot of the competitors get sorted out in the preliminaries, but some pretty good material survives for the semi-finals and finals.'

'If by some extraordinary chance Caroline gets as far as that I expect I shall watch on television,' said Aunt Hilda thoughtfully. 'Unless it's more than my nerves will stand.'

'If she reached the finals,' replied Jeremy, obviously speaking more or less in joke, 'you could go to the actual performance. It will be open to the public, and I'm sure there would be reserved seats for relatives and friends.'

'Oh, I couldn't do that,' declared Aunt Hilda seriously. 'That *would* be more than my nerves could take.'

Fortunately years with Aunt Hilda had armoured Caroline against feelings of hurt and pride. But she was glad when, the next day at the office, Dinah referred to a TV announcement about the impending Contest and said admiringly, 'I felt proud to know someone who was actually going in. You *are* going in, aren't you?'

'Oh, yes. I'm quite determined about that. For several reasons,' Caroline added, half to herself, which made Dinah cock an interested glance at her and ask,

'What does Mr Marshall think about it?'

'I don't know that he's specially interested,' replied Caroline most untruthfully.

'Oh, he *must* be! Imagine someone in his own

office making a splash like that. I mean if you scooped up one of the prizes. He'd offer himself as your agent on the spot—and you'd just have to accept, wouldn't you?'

'I might not,' said Caroline, thinking of Lucille. 'He already has a number of sopranos on his list.'

'But——' Dinah's jaw dropped slightly'—you couldn't have a better agent, and he'd be bound to give you special treatment. As a matter of fact, I've sometimes thought he's a bit keen on you. Haven't you?'

'No, I have not.' Caroline's tone was emphatic. 'Which is just as well——' she managed a slight laugh'—because I've heard rumours that he's either engaged or about to be.'

'Oh, too bad,' declared Dinah cheerfully. 'Bang goes another romantic dream!' And she turned back to her typewriter, while Caroline swallowed an unexpected lump in her throat.

Ken came back the following day, but she managed to be out of the office for the day—in the morning at the Opera Studio and later with Sir Oscar.

'Here are the particulars about your precious Carruthers Contest and your entry form,' said Warrender, handing over a sheaf of papers. 'If not with my total approval, at least with my cordial good wishes.'

She examined them thoughtfully, then, without raising her head, she asked in a low voice, 'What are my chances, Sir Oscar?'

'I couldn't even hazard a guess,' was the reply. 'There are too many varying factors involved. For one thing, we don't yet know who the judges will be. Oh, reputable, of course, and distinguished in their own field, no doubt. But even in the higher reaches of our profession different people are looking for different qualities.'

'How do you mean?'

'Well, academics are, quite legitimately, looking for academic excellence. Old professionals like myself look for something more original, more personally and musically arresting. While the occasional patron or official or what-have-you is entitled to back his or her own fancy, within the terms of reference.'

'I wish you were on the jury,' said Caroline with a sigh.

'If I were, either you or I would have to withdraw,' he assured her. 'It wouldn't be ethical, you know, for one of the judges to have had a hand in training one of the competitors.'

'I hadn't thought of that!' She looked taken aback. 'But if you *were* on the jury, Sir Oscar, what sort of rating would you give me?'

'Without an opportunity to assess the other competitors, how can I tell?'

She thought that was all he was prepared to say. But he went on slowly, 'In my view, however, the winners of the first three prizes are going to have to be very good indeed to displace you.'

'Thank you!' She smiled brilliantly. Though she added obstinately, 'But it has to be the *first* prize.'

'If it's any help to you, I've heard that one of the judges may well be Enid Mountjoy, and she will certainly be looking for what I would describe as the right things. She's no longer young, but her judgment is excellent,' he stated authoritatively. 'She was responsible for quite a lot of Anthea's training, incidentally.'

'By your arrangement?' Caroline asked interestedly.

'By my arrangement,' he confirmed, and somehow that was very cheering.

The next day she went to the office dreading the first meeting with Ken. If he were to impart to her the news of his engagement in some offhand manner she hardly knew how she could take it with decent composure. But she was not put to the test. Apparently his private affairs were not for discussion between them.

He breezed into the office, full of information about some successful contracts, but also, it seemed, very willing for further discussion about the evening in Warrender's studio when he had heard her sing.

'My critical godmother is going to be very gratified when she hears you and realises she's backed a winner,' he informed her with a mischievous smile, and she suddenly wanted to hit him for continuing the masquerade with such gusto.

'Do you think so?' Her tone was cool.

'Yes. Don't you?'

'I hope so—naturally,' she replied indifferently, and went over to the filing cabinet so that she could turn her back on him.

'What's the matter?' His voice changed suddenly. 'And don't say "Nothing",' he added irritably before she could.

'What would you like me to say, then?' She had never spoken to him in that tone before, and she could feel the cloud of astonishment behind her.

'Turn round and look at me,' he said quietly, and when she took no notice she heard him get up and cross the room. The next moment he had swung her round to face him and, shifting his grip, he held her by her upper arms so that she was almost against him.

'What's this charade in aid of?' he asked, and for the first time she was surprisedly aware of a note of brutality in his voice.

'I don't know what you're talking about!' and her voice shook with anger and pain as she tried, unavailingly, to escape from his grip. 'Let go of me, please. I don't like employers who take liberties.'

'Liberties? Good God, girl, you don't know what the word means! But if you want to know——' and before she could stop him, he bent his head and kissed her hard on her angry mouth with a sort of brutal deliberation which made her gasp.

'You—skunk! I suppose you think that spending a fortune on me without my knowledge entitles you to maul me?'

He fell away from her as though she had literally struck him.

'So that's the trouble? You've found out I'm paying for your training.'

It was as good a way out as any, she supposed, with her heart like lead. She had so nearly betrayed her fury and misery over Lucille's conquest. Better a thousand times that he should think she resented his spending money on her and keeping her in ignorance of the fact.

'You knew I would never have accepted if you'd been frank with me, didn't you? But in your arrogance you made this ridiculous plot with your godmother and took the decision out of my hands.'

'Oh, stop being a melodramatic little fool!' he exclaimed impatiently. 'Can't a man make a generous gesture to his own secretary without being suspected of what used to be called base designs? You're in the wrong century, Caroline.'

She said nothing, and after a moment he asked almost sullenly, 'How did you find out?'

'It doesn't matter.' She spoke rather wearily, because suddenly the fire had gone out of her and the taste of ashes was in her mouth. 'You needn't blame anyone, Ken——' the familiar form of address slipped out without her noticing '—I did a bit of inspired guessing, and no one tried to deny that I'd arrived at the right conclusion. Even if you meant it all for the best, it's something which gives me no satisfaction. Please let's leave the subject now.'

'At least let me apologise.' He thrust his hands into his pockets and frowned at the floor.

'For forcing your money on me?'

'No, of course not. I have no regrets about that. For kissing you the way I did.'

'As though I were some cheap little office girl who might like it, you mean?'

'I've said I'm sorry,' he exclaimed angrily.

'I accept that. And now—forget it.' Caroline gave a slight shrug as though the whole incident were too distasteful to discuss further.

He turned and went back to his desk without a word, and she thought, with a strange pain at her heart, that she had never before seen him robbed of his self-assurance.

When she went back to her own office Dinah was typing with her usual speed and gusto. But she stopped at once and remarked, 'You've been a long time. Were you discussing the Carruthers business?'

Caroline shook her head and said, unblushingly, that they had been discussing office matters.

'And he didn't tell you about his engagement?' Dinah was obviously a little disappointed.

'Of course not, Dinah! His private affairs are no concern of mine.'

'Strictly speaking, no. But then you're good friends outside the office, aren't you? You can't go to all those performances together and not be on friendly out-of-office terms. So it wouldn't be unusual if he told you about anything as important as an engagement.' Caroline said nothing and Dinah went on, 'Perhaps he'll tell you this evening. You're going to the opera tonight, aren't you?'

'Tonight?' Caroline sounded dismayed. 'I'd forgotten.'

'You'd *forgotten* that you're going to "Eugene Onegin", with Nicholas Brenner singing Lensky? You don't deserve to have a free seat,' declared Dinah. 'Unless—oh, I suppose you're getting jumpy about the Carruthers Contest,' she added indulgently. 'Don't worry so much, Caroline. From all accounts you'll make a good showing, and no one is expecting you to carry off the top prize.'

'*I* am expecting myself to carry off the top

prize,' replied Caroline huskily. 'And what do you mean when you say "from all accounts" I'll make a good showing? From whose account, for goodness' sake?'

'Well, from Mr Marshall's account, to tell the truth,' Dinah admitted. 'He heard you the other evening, didn't he? He was telling me about it yesterday, and he said you were quite wonderful—that you actually brought a lump into his experienced throat. He was laughing, of course, but I think he half meant it.'

'He likes to throw off remarks like that,' Caroline said curtly. 'They don't mean anything.'

'Why, Caroline, I don't know what's got into you this morning!' Dinah was genuinely astonished. 'You've certainly got your knife into poor old K.M.' And she turned back to her work with a dismissive shrug.

By the time Caroline met him that evening in the vestibule at Covent Garden she had determined that they must return to some sort of normal relationship. So she greeted him with a smile and said, 'Let me start by apologising for being so silly and unreasonable this morning—and then forget it, if you will.'

He looked immensely relieved and replied, 'My opening exactly, if you hadn't got in first. It wasn't the best morning for either of us, was it?'

She shook her head, and he went on, 'As for my—gaffe in trying to play generous patron without consulting you, I hope you will acquit me of any unworthy motives.'

He said that half laughingly, but his eyes were serious. And when she replied, 'Forget it—forget it,' he was not to know that it was pain and not impatience which sharpened her voice.

In other circumstances he might have referred again to the impression her voice had made on him in Warrender's studio, but possibly he felt that would take them a little too near to the root cause of their difference that morning. At any rate, he made no further comment about her voice or his reaction to it.

Instead, it was she who floated a provocative opening in the first interval, by saying casually, 'I expect you know that Jeremy is going back to Germany almost immediately on a renewed contract.'

'Yes, of course. I'm glad for him. He's a nice chap and a gifted one. If he works hard and has a bit of luck he should make the grade all right. I suppose he's feeling pretty good at the moment?'

'Oh, he is. Even though,' she added deliberately, 'Lucille Duparc has given him the brush-off.'

'It was inevitable,' he said, almost without interest. 'Lucille is not the woman to complicate her life and career with a struggling young tenor.'

'You mean,' Caroline spoke coolly, 'that she was after bigger fish?'

'Oh, definitely,' he said, laughed. But before she could react to that he said, 'Excuse me—there's Farraday. I want a word with him.' And he left her, sitting there feeling comfortless and troubled.

Presently, however, one of her fellow students from the Opera Studio joined her, bringing with her an evening paper containing a short article on the Carruthers Contest. It contained also a list of the judges, and on this Caroline fastened with painful eagerness.

'Keep the paper,' said her friend generously. 'It's of more interest to you than to me, though we'll all be wishing you luck, of course.'

'Thank you,' said Caroline and, glancing down at the article, she saw that Enid Mountjoy was among the judges.

When Ken returned she had time to show him the article before the orchestra started coming back, and he said immediately, 'Enid Mountjoy, I see. Good! She has our set of values. Hm—hm—Anthony Graveney—marvellous instrumentalist but knows little about singing. Very prestigious in his own field, of course. I suppose that's why they invited him.'

'And the others?' Caroline's voice was anxious.

He ran his finger down the list, commenting. 'That one represents money, of course, and fancies himself as a patron of the arts—oh, dear! we could have done without *her*. But let's hope someone intelligent like Enid sways her vote. Those three are quite good judges in a cautious way. As for the others—a pretty routine lot, Caroline. If Enid does her stuff and is sweetly authoritiative we should gather in some of the floating voters. A lot depends on her.'

During the second act Caroline strove to concentrate on the performance and forget the newspaper article. This became instantly much easier when Nicholas Brenner was on the stage; and when, as the ardent but doomed Lensky, he sang his lovely farewell to life, it was quite impossible to think about the Carruthers Contest or anything else.

'It's all so *Russian*,' commented someone sitting behind Caroline. 'Why on earth couldn't they have got together and had a little plain speaking? It would have saved such a lot of trouble.'

'But lost us some superb music,' countered her annoyed escort very truly. Caroline found herself exchanging a smile with Ken, and for a moment it was as though their previous happy relationship were restored.

She would not, however, allow him to escort her home. By good fortune she ran into her friend from the Opera Studio again and, knowing she lived in much the same direction as herself, Caroline insisted on joining her.

It seemed that everyone in the next few weeks spoke of little but the Carruthers Contest. Newspaper comment was continual, fellow students were loud in their generous good wishes, Aunt Hilda said it upset her nerves just to think of it, and Jeremy took himself off to Germany, his hopes for his own affairs high and his advice to his cousin both affectionate and cautious.

'I should hate you to be cruelly disappointed,' he said sincerely. 'Even to make the semi-finals would be fine for anyone at your stage of development——' he had somehow not been able to make time to hear her or assess any progress she had made'—so be happy, Carrie dear, if you get a certificate of merit.'

Caroline said she would, though she had no intention whatever of being satisfied with any old certificate of merit.

As is usual in many contests, the competitors were divided into groups of six, and the winners of each group went on to compete with each other. From these, the twelve best would then progress to the semi-finals, where six would be weeded out. The remaining six then went forward to the finals.

Unexpectedly, Caroline found herself petrified with fright at the very first 'heat', and was genuinely surprised when she was unhesitatingly chosen as the winner of her group.

'I thought I should die,' she told Aunt Hilda, who replied,

'I thought I should too, sitting here alone at home, wondering what was happening. Thank goodness this early trial wasn't televised. I'm glad you won, dear, but I don't know what I'm going to do if you go on to further stages.'

'I don't know what I'm going to do if I *don't*!' replied Caroline, with a laugh.

'Well, don't be too self-confident,' said Aunt Hilda. 'And you might just go and turn out the oven. I think I smell something burning.'

It was not until the next round—what might be called the quarter finals—that it was obvious how stiff the competition was going to be. At this point the judging was taken over by the distinguished panel who would continue to the end. This was therefore the first time Caroline saw Enid Mountjoy, and immediately her hopes rose.

Not by the slightest sign, of course, did the distinguished elderly lady at the end of the row indicate any sort of preference. But, by that indefinable, almost psychic wave which can pass between two people, Caroline knew she had made her mark.

At the end she found herself among the twelve

who were to go forward to the semi-finals. She also found herself for the first time in her life being interviewed by an enthusiastic journalist who said emphatically, 'You're a winner!'

She felt splendid, until she overheard him saying the same thing to another competitor, so that when she came to be photographed she was looking very solemn indeed.

'It doesn't flatter you,' Aunt Hilda said disparagingly as she regarded the rather smudgy result. 'Remember to *smile* if you get as far as being televised.'

Caroline, who felt she would never smile again, had no further comment to make.

There was a gap of a week before the semi-finals, during which Caroline—and presumably the other contestants too—went through a veritable hell of conflicting hopes and fears.

'There's no need to panic at this stage,' Oscar Warrender told her in a disagreeable but oddly bracing way. 'People who succumb to nerves on the third rung of the ladder seldom reach the top—which is where your talents should take you eventually, even if you win nothing in this wretched contest.'

'I can't *bear* it if I win nothing,' cried Caroline.

'You may have no choice,' was the chilling reply. 'In our profession we have to learn to bear a lot of things. Endurance is an essential part of becoming an artist. Remember that.'

'I'll try, I'll try,' Caroline promised. 'And I think Enid Mountjoy is in my favour.'

'What makes you think that?' enquired Warrender with interest.

'Something—indefinable,' Caroline admitted.

'She didn't smile—at least no more than politely, as she did to all of us. But there's something about her sheer presence which reassures me.'

'Then sing specially for her,' Warrender said not unkindly.

So during the semi-finals Caroline sang specially for Enid Mountjoy. And at the end she dazedly heard her name among the six chosen to go forward to the finals, which were to take place in public before a large audience, with full TV coverage.

'Now I shall *have* to watch,' lamented Aunt Hilda. 'I don't know how I can!'

Caroline suggested that it was more harrowing for the contestants, but Aunt Hilda would not have that.

'Oh, I don't know. At least all six of you will get something for your ordeal, I suppose.'

'A copper bowl and a certificate,' said Caroline crossly and ungratefully, but Aunt Hilda said how nice a copper bowl would look on the sideboard.

The finals were to take place on Friday, in the splendid hall of St Cecilia's Music College, famous for its superb acoustics and the fact that it could seat over a thousand people. Then on Wednesday the most extraordinary thing happened. Aunt Hilda presented Caroline with a hundred pounds and told her to go and buy a pretty dress for the occasion.

'Aunt Hilda!' Caroline was touched almost to tears. 'You *darling*! You shouldn't have—but oh, I'm so glad that you did! I didn't really want to wear my old white one.'

'Certainly not! White looks wishy-washy on

the screen. I couldn't have that. I waited to see if your mysterious patron was going to provide you with a dress for the occasion, but it appears not.'

'Oh, he couldn't, you know!'

'*He?*' Aunt Hilda looked outraged. 'You always said it was a she. Do you mean you've been taking money from some strange man all this time?'

'No, no! Not exactly that.'

'How old is he?' asked Aunt Hilda inexorably.

And Caroline, crossing her fingers and hoping the Recording Angel was looking the other way, said he was seventy-two.

'Oh, well——' Aunt Hilda was mollified and the moment of crisis passed. But it seemed that the Recording Angel had not been looking the other way, because retribution followed as swift as thought.

'Here's a bit more about the contest,' observed Aunt Hilda, glancing at the evening paper which had just arrived. 'There's a change in the panel of judges. One of them is ill and has to be replaced.'

'*Which* one?' Caroline almost snatched the paper, and then gave a gasp of dismay. 'It's Enid Mountjoy.——Oh, it can't be! She—she won't be there. Oh, what shall I do?'

'Don't be silly.' Her aunt took back the paper into her own keeping. 'It will be someone else just as good. It says so here. "She will be replaced by a judge of equal distinction".'

'It's not the same thing!' Caroline's voice registered complete tragedy, and suddenly she did something she would never have contemplated in any other circumstances. She went to the telephone and dialled the Warrenders' number.

It was the housekeeper who answered and she said, 'They're both out, Miss Caroline. They won't be home until late.'

'Thank you.' Slowly Caroline replaced the receiver. Then after a pause she picked it up again even more slowly and dialled another number. Almost immediately Kennedy Marshall's voice replied.

'Ken! It's Caroline. Have you seen the evening paper?'

'Yes. But I knew about Enid Mountjoy's illness earlier in the day. Don't worry too much, Caroline. They're bound to get someone very——'

'But *she* is the one I was counting on. She liked me—I know she did. She gave me confidence in a way I can't describe. It may sound silly, but I felt we—understood each other. You need someone like that when your courage is slipping.'

He made no reply to that, and after a moment, she asked, 'How did you know earlier in the day?'

'They applied to me—I suppose they tried other agents too—to see if I could suggest anyone on my books.'

'And couldn't you?'

There was an infinitesimal pause, and then he said, 'No, I'm afraid I couldn't. I had to tell them so.' And there seemed no more to say.

Back with Aunt Hilda Caroline tried to hide her nervous anxiety—to concentrate on the generous gift of the dress (as near as possible to the colour of her eyes, Aunt Hilda advised), but she shook with fear every time she saw herself facing that line of judges with no Enid Mountjoy to sustain her courage.

The next day she went to buy the dress, to which Aunt Hilda quite justifiably attached almost more importance than to the contest itself. As though by prior arrangement she discovered what in other circumstances she would have regarded as the dress of her dreams. It was the exact shade Aunt Hilda had advised, and cut on such simple and subtle lines that it was grace and charm personified.

Caroline knew she had never looked so lovely in her life. But she would have willingly traded the most glorious dress in the world for the secure knowledge that somehow Enid Mountjoy would, by some miracle, be present on the jury after all.

Later in the day she went through the few items she had chosen to sing on the morrow, and Anthea at least tried to reassure her that all would be well. Warrender characteristically offered no such easy reassurance.

'I realise it's a major blow for you, Caroline,' he said. 'But long before you're at the top of your profession you will have learned that these are the heart shaking emergencies we have to contend with. You're a gifted girl and a courageous girl. Don't disappoint me by allowing cowardice to ruin everything. I believe in you—and you must justify that belief.'

Then, to her immeasurable surprise, he kissed her before passing her on to Anthea's affectionate embrace.

'Good luck, darling,' said Anthea. 'And remember—you didn't find my diamond ring for nothing. That was fate, that was!'

Throughout the next twenty-four hours

Caroline clung to the words of support she had received in the Warrenders' flat. And when, dressed in the beautiful violet-blue dress so unexpectedly provided by Aunt Hilda, she was ready to leave for the scene of battle, she knew she had never before looked so arresting. Nor—she really had to admit it with all modesty—more lovely.

'It's most becoming, Caroline!' Her aunt circled round her with beaming complacence. 'I'm so glad I thought of it. The shoddy white one wouldn't have done at all. I really *will* look in tonight. I'll make myself do it——' she spoke as though making up her mind to visit the dentist '—Mrs Corrigan said I must make the effort, and her son is going to fetch me in next door.'

Caroline praised her courage and resolution, as though it were Aunt Hilda who was to battle her way to success or failure that evening. Then she drove away in the hired car which her employer had insisted on providing when she refused to let him drive her in person.

'It will make me more nervous to be with someone I know,' she had said, and he had accepted that.

Backstage in the hall the place was crowded and the atmosphere tense. Technicians were holding microphones or trailing wires, producers and assistant producers were issuing directions, competitors appeared from time to time at their dressing-room doors, to receive bouquets from management or well-wishers. They also exchanged sickly smiles and tried not to hate each other.

A young assistant director who had complimented Caroline more than once during the early stages of the contest informed her encouragingly that the hall was filling up splendidly.

'Do you want to come and see for yourself?' he asked. 'There's a convenient peephole at the side of the stage.'

She shook her head and said it might make her even more nervous.

'It wouldn't, you know,' he reassured her. 'In a way it's better to receive the impact of the scene *before* you actually make your entrance to sing. Then you don't have the shock of finding that perhaps it's different from what you've visualised.'

That seemed good sense, and Caroline accompanied him to the side of the stage.

'A little more this way,' he directed her. 'I think that applause means that the judges are coming in.'

'Oh——' She immediately applied her eye to the peephole, eager to see the people who held her fate in their hands. For a moment it was difficult to focus. Then, as the complete scene swung into view and she saw the judges moving in, she let out an audible gasp. For the distinguished substitute for Enid Mountjoy was Lucille Duparc.

CHAPTER EIGHT

FOR a few moments Caroline remained perfectly still, as though continuing to examine the hall. Then, when she judged that her expression had become normal, she turned to the friendly director and said,

'Thank you very much. That was a good idea of yours. I shan't be so taken aback now when I go onstage and face the hall for the first time.'

He wished her luck once more and she went to her dressing-room, sat down in the one comfortable armchair and deliberately tried to relax.

'I'm not going to let it shake me,' she told herself, but she clenched her hands until the knuckles went white with the effort to control her fury. 'She arranged it! Lucille arranged it—and Ken backed her up, although he knew it was the last thing I would want. She talked him over and he did it to please her, even though he must have known it would shake my nerves to see her there.'

No wonder he had been evasive about the search for a substitute for Enid Mountjoy! After that tiny pause in their telephone conversation he had said he had been unable to suggest anyone. But Lucille Duparc, whose agent he was, had replaced Enid Mountjoy. She was sitting there now in the hall, waiting to pass judgment on the contestants—one of whom she disliked intensely.

'I despise her for a snake in the grass,' thought Caroline bitterly. 'But I despise him even more for being her tool. And *I will not be defeated*!'

She spread out her hands in front of her and saw to her astonishment that they displayed not the slightest tremor. An almost frozen composure possessed her, though beneath that calm there was a raging fire of fury.

She would show them!—all of them: Her friends and supporters, from Oscar Warrender to Dinah Gale, seated somewhere up there in the balcony. The judges, from the most impartial to the most easily swayed. Her enemies—Lucille Duparc who wished her ill and Kennedy Marshall whom she could have loved but who had betrayed her.

Anything so paltry as quivering nerves entered not at all into her mood of the moment. The reserved and self-effacing girl who had once been the least forceful of Aunt Hilda's household had disappeared. Not instantaneously, of course, but in the gradual build-up of the dedicated artist, in the dawning awareness of the loving girl. Now the raging force of the injured woman fused all those elements into an irresistible force.

She was no longer afraid of either judges or public. She was out to inflict ignominious defeat on the two people who had combined to snatch triumph from her.

Caroline's place was fourth in the evening's programme. On the intercom in her dressing-room she listened, appreciatively but unafraid, to the first three, all of whom were unquestionably of a high standard. When she was finally summoned to take her place in the wings, preparatory to making her own entry on the stage, she did of course experience a slight qualm. But, as she walked on to the stage, erect and graceful in Aunt Hilda's beautiful dress, Oscar Warrender muttered instantly to his wife,

'Something has happened to her. She's in command of her own destiny.'

She stood there, calm and self-possessed, while the orchestra played the introduction to 'Divinités du Styx', Gluck's great aria for Alceste in which she appeals to the gods of the Underworld to release her husband; then she took the opening phrases like a high-grade professional.

There was anguished pleading in the tones of Caroline's beautiful, well-schooled voice, but there was also an irresistible strength of purpose. This was an Alceste who knew the power of her own love and believed that the gods themselves would not be able to refuse her.

'*How* old is she?' murmured someone seated behind the Warrenders, then, having obviously consulted the note in the programme, 'Twenty-three? I don't believe it.'

There was a moment of stunned silence at the end of the aria, and then prolonged applause. Caroline smiled charmingly, but did not deign even to glance in the direction of Lucille.

Then she gave a little nod to the conductor and, in almost startling contrast to the pure lines of the Gluck aria, she sang 'Senza Mamma', the touching lament of the sinning little nun in Puccini's 'Suor Angelica' for the dead child she has never been allowed to see.

Melodically this is one of the composer's most beautiful inspirations. Emotionally it can tremble on the edge of lush sentiment unless impeccably sung. Indeed, Warrender had been very doubtful about letting Caroline do it. But that evening she could not put a foot wrong. Faultlessly she trod the golden tightrope between sentiment and true pathos.

At the end Dinah was not the only one to shed tears, Warrender said, 'She's home and dry unless we have a genius among the last two,' and Kennedy Marshall watched her leave the stage without even attempting to applaud her.

'Well done!' the friendly assistant director was once more beside Caroline. 'Do you know that you sang twice as well as at the rehearsal?'

'Thank you.' She smiled gratefully at him. 'I felt very relaxed.'

'*Relaxed?* When this was the supreme test? How come?'

'I don't know,' replied Caroline tranquilly. But she knew all right.

All the same, she felt slightly sick when the moment came for them all to return to the stage and hear the results.

There was a long, and totally unappreciated, speech from the chairman of the company about the duty of successful enterprises to support the arts, the gratitude everyone felt towards the distinguished judges who had given so generously of their time and expertise, etc., etc.

Then he explained that the prize-winners would be announced in the reverse order of success. This enabled the three runners-up to be presented with their copper bowls and certificates—and take a step back from the centre of mounting interest.

The third prize—quite a handsome cheque—

went to a very promising baritone, who was obviously delighted.

'I can't *bear* it!' whispered Anthea to her husband.

'Relax. It's all right,' he replied, taking her hand. And all right it was.

The second prize was awarded to a well-schooled but slightly uninteresting mezzo-soprano, amidst much applause—which registered not only good wishes towards her but instense relief that there was now only one competitor left to take the first prize.

When that was presented to Caroline the display of enthusiasm and applause almost rocked the hall, and showed very clearly who was the popular favourite.

She accepted the cheque, the copper bowl which was going to look so nice on Aunt Hilda's sideboard, and the kiss bestowed upon her by the chairman's wife. Then she stepped forward and, with a charming composure not to have been even thought of six months ago, she expressed her thanks to all concerned—and smiled straight at Lucille Duparc.

More applause followed and, now that most of the audience were standing, Caroline was able to pick out some familiar figures. She raised her hand in affectionate respect to the Warrenders and Mrs Van Kroll, waved to the upper reaches of the hall from which came ecstatic cries of, 'Caroline!' indicating fellow students and Dinah Gale. To the almost weeping Miss Curtis she blew a smiling kiss, and then she left the stage, having apparently not seen Kennedy Marshall standing applauding very near the front.

Backstage there was much photographing, television filming, questions and comments from journalists, and congratulations from some of the judges. Lucille Duparc was not among the last, nor did the absence of Ken Marshall surprise Caroline.

Amid a certain amount of respectful interest, the Warrenders came round to congratulate her, and a bold journalist asked, 'What do you think of her, Sir Oscar?'

'The same as you all do, judging by the applause,' the conductor replied diplomatically, and prepared to leave with his wife before Anthea could do much more than hug Caroline and whisper, 'I was right about the ring, wasn't I? It was *fate*!'

'Where's the boss?' Dinah wanted to know, having now made her way through the crowd to Caroline.

'Somewhere around, I imagine,' was the careless reply.

'Ready with an open contract in his hand, I should think,' replied Dinah exultantly, whereas Sir Oscar suddenly turned back to Caroline and said sternly, 'No contracts, signatures, offers, gifts or suggestions without consulting me, remember.'

'Of course not, Sir Oscar!'

'Not even offers of marriage?' added Dinah, getting a bit above herself.

'That least of all,' replied Warrender drily as he and his wife left.

The rest of the evening was a sort of confused whirl of exicted impressions. There was the celebration banquet, with more flowers, more

speeches, more compliments, the parrying of
Press enquiries about future plans, the cautious
half-promise to appear on television—but only
with Warrender's full permission.

'He directs all my studies and activities, you
know,' she stated firmly, and she heard someone
observe, 'Then she must indeed be a winner in
every respect.'

At last, bone-weary, sick with a sense of
reaction, and suddenly overwhelmed by the most
ghastly depression which she could not possibly
explain to herself, she made her final excuses and
escaped.

Gratefully she sank into the blessed darkness of
a taxi, whose driver was fortunately totally
unaware that he was driving the heroine of the
evening. He did, however comment on the wealth
of flowers she was carrying as she got out at her
home, and on a sudden impulse she asked, 'Have
you a wife at home?'

'Not at home,' was the wry reply. 'But she'll be
coming back from hospital next week, with the
baby.'

'Oh, please take her some of these flowers,'
cried Caroline. 'Take her these——' she thrust
into his arms the three dozen roses from which
she had just detached a card with Ken's name
written upon it. 'I'd like her to have them.'

'But they're the pick of the bunch! Don't you
want——'

'No!' she said almost feverishly. 'No, I'd rather
she had them,' and she pressed the flowers upon
him. Then she dropped the card in the gutter,
turned away, deaf to his thanks, and went into the
house with the tears running down her cheeks.

Aunt Hilda for once did not call out, 'Is that you, Caroline?' She rushed into the hall, flung her arms round her niece with more energy than she had displayed in years, and cried, 'The dress looked *wonderful* and you were splendid too. Why are you crying?'

'I'm tired, Auntie—I'm tired. It's the reaction, I suppose. I'll be all right in a minute.' Caroline wiped away the tears with the backs of her hands. 'Here's your copper bowl. It's rather nice, isn't it?'

'It's lovely,' declared Aunt Hilda appreciatively, as she set it on the sideboard. 'They did the whole thing excellently on TV, and when they ran the cameras along the row of judges I thought the one who replaced your friend looked charming. Such a sweet, earnest expression. Who was she?'

'She was Lucille Duparc, and I hate her guts,' replied Caroline.

Aunt Hilda, who did not approve of expressions like that, said automatically, 'Don't be vulgar, dear. Why don't you like her? Because she was unkind to Jeremy?'

'No,' said Caroline slowly. 'Oh, no. That's all so long ago in the past.' At which Aunt Hilda looked at her a little anxiously and said,

'You're losing sense of time. You'd better go to bed and rest. It's all been too much for you. I know it was for me too. Would you like some hot milk in bed?'

'No, thank you, Auntie. Would you?'

'Well, you know, I think I would,' replied Aunt Hilda. 'It's been a terribly exhausting evening.'

So she went to bed, and Caroline brought her some hot milk and even sat on the end of the bed and talked a little more, this time with great self-possession and even a touch of humour. Then, as she was leaving, she said,

'I'm going to stay late in bed tomorrow. I need to re-charge the batteries.'

'You do just that,' agreed Aunt Hilda, adding with a sigh of relief, 'Mrs Glass will be here in the morning and will see to everything. Sleep well.'

And the extraordinary thing was that Caroline did. She had expected to lie awake for hours, going over the events of the evening in retrospect. Above all, she had intended to put Ken's behaviour under the microscope of her contemptuous judgment. But instead she put her head on the pillow and slept dreamlessly until the sound of the telephone roused her.

'It's for you, Miss Caroline——' Mrs Glass knocked on the door to summon her. And, with some confused idea that it might be Ken, she roused herself and went to the telephone.

It was not of course Ken. It was the director of an Italian film company, asking for the name of her agent.

'I haven't got an agent,' said Caroline, and smothered a yawn.

'You have no agent?' The voice at the other end sounded incredulous and excited. 'Then may I recommend you to a very distinguished one? He is internationally famous and has worked with me on many films. If I might——'

'Thank you, but—no.' By now Caroline had come fully to the surface. 'I do nothing without consulting Sir Oscar Warrender or——'

She stopped at that point, very suddenly, and quietly hung up the receiver, for she realised that she had very nearly added Ken's name as someone who might be consulted about her professional affairs. The shock of rediscovering the wretched truth brought a fresh wave of pain, and she stood there in the hall remembering how they had laughed together and agreed that he would be her agent.

But that was long, long ago. Not in time but in the story of their relationship.

There were a good many other telephone calls during that Saturday, all of them congratulatory, many of them truly affectionate. But there was nothing from Ken.

She was not really expecting to hear from him, of course. He must know quite well, from her deliberate avoidance of him the previous evening, that she now knew how it was that Lucille had come to be one of the judges. Consequently he surely realised that this was the end of any friendship between him and her.

'Will you be going to the office on Monday?' Aunt Hilda wanted to know. 'I suppose in the circumstances you could have the day off if you wanted it?'

'I suppose I could,' Caroline agreed. 'But I shall look in some time during the morning. There's something I have to settle.'

'With Mr Marshall?' Aunt Hilda looked curious, perhaps because of her niece's tone.

'With Mr Marshall,' Caroline agreed, and changed the subject.

Sunday was, predictably, a quieter day than

Saturday, but Miss Curtis called during the afternoon.

'I shall not stay long,' she explained to Aunt Hilda. 'But I just had to come in and congratulate dear Caroline once more.'

'Of course.' Aunt Hilda inclined her head with gracious understanding, already perfecting her role as close relative of the famous. And she left Caroline and her teacher together.

'Sophie was as thrilled as any of us,' Miss Curtis assured Caroline. 'Indeed, she was so delighted that I ventured to confess last night that I'd told you the truth some while ago. She forgave me on the spot and said she was sure that her godson wouldn't mind now.'

'He doesn't mind,' said Caroline tonelessly. 'I told him myself.'

'Last night?' Miss Curtis looked most intrigued.

'No, no. Quite a long time ago.'

There was an odd little silence, then Miss Curtis said, 'It couldn't be a *long* time ago, dear. You didn't know yourself until quite recently.'

'No, that's true. It—seems a long time. Everything has changed so much.'

'Of course, of course,' Miss Curtis agreed sympathetically. 'It must seem as though your whole life has changed since last night. Well, of course it *has*.'

'Yes, it has all changed,' said Caroline in such an odd voice that her old teacher looked at her sharply and rose to go.

'You still need to rest, Caroline. Don't go to the office tomorrow or——'

'I have to go. There's something I must settle,' replied Caroline just as she had to Aunt Hilda.

'Won't it wait?'

'No,' said Caroline. 'It won't wait.'

And Miss Curtis, whose ear was sensitively attuned to the tones of the human voice, felt oddly perturbed as she took her leave.

According to Aunt Hilda, however, Caroline looked much more herself the next day. She even laughed quite gaily as she announced, 'I'm going in triumph to the bank on my way to the office, to deposit my famous cheque.'

'They'll be impressed,' declared Aunt Hilda. And impressed they were, for it is not every day that a customer wins three thousand pounds just by singing two arias. Indeed, one junior clerk actually asked for her autograph.

'So long as it's not on a cheque,' replied Caroline, and she left the bank smiling like a girl who had not a care in the world.

Dinah welcomed her with fresh congratulations and a dozen new questions, so that they talked for ten minutes or more before Dinah, recollecting the right order of things, exclaimed,

'Mr Marshall came in half an hour ago! I mustn't keep you gossiping. He probably wants to talk it all over with you himself.'

Caroline nodded, abstracted a slip of paper from her handbag and, crossing the passage to Ken Marshall's office, she knocked.

'Come in.'

He looked up as she entered and, inexplicably, it hurt her that his expression was unsure— almost wary.

'Hello!' He had recovered himself. 'Congratulations on your triumph, since I didn't get a chance to speak to you on the great evening. I hardly expected to see you this morning. You'd earned the day off, I'd have thought.'

'But I had to see you about something.'

'Oh?—About what?'

For answer she put the slip of paper on his desk in front of him and just stood there waiting.

He picked it up and after a moment she saw, with something like horror, that it was shaking in his hands.

'What's this?' His voice was quite low and a little hoarse. Then he looked up at her, those bright grey eyes as cold as a winter's dawn.

'As you see——' it took a great effort to keep her voice steady '—it's a blank cheque from me to you. I should be glad if you would fill it in for the amount you've spent on my training.'

There was quite a long pause. Then he said slowly, and still with his glance upon her, 'You heartless little jade!' and he tore the cheque across and then across again.

Caroline thought for a moment that he was going to fling the pieces at her, but instead he put them in a neat pile before him on his desk with hands that were still unsteady.

'You must understand——' she began more uncertainly than she had intended.

'I understand perfectly,' he told her. 'I understand that for the first time in my life I've made a fool of myself about a woman. A conceited, heartless girl who——'

A knock on the door interrupted him and Dinah entered to announce brightly, 'Excuse me, Mr Marshall, but Miss Lucille Duparc is on the phone.'

'Who?' He looked at Dinah as though he had forgotten who she was.

'Lucille Duparc,' said Dinah more uncertainly as she realised that the moment was not exactly propitious. 'What shall I tell her?'

'Tell her,' said Kennedy Marshall slowly, 'to go to hell.'

'In those exact words, Mr Marshall?'

'In those exact words. And you can add for good measure that I no longer represent her.'

'All right,' said Dinah, and withdrew, her manner subtly suggesting that the task was not displeasing to her.

There was a long silence. Then Caroline sat down on the other side of the desk because her legs suddenly felt as though they were made of cotton wool.

'Ken,' she said huskily, then she cleared her throat and started again. 'Ken, what made you send such a message to Lucille? Have you—quarrelled with her or something?'

'Quarrelled?' He looked faintly puzzled. 'You don't *quarrel* with the Lucilles of this world. You just string along with them professionally speaking, taking care they don't contrive to mix pleasure with business. But it's totally unimportant. Why are we discussing her?'

She stared at him in dismayed silence and he went on with an impatient sigh, 'You'd better go, my dear. There isn't anything left for us to say to each other, is there? If you want to write your resignation now, I accept it. But——' suddenly he swept the pieces of the cheque from his desk '—that I will never accept, in any circumstances whatever.'

'Why not?' She spoke in a whisper.

He got up and went to the window, where he

stood staring out, his back to her, so that she thought he was not going to give her any sort of reply. Then, still without turning, he said slowly in a voice she had never heard from him before,

'Something offered with love should never be rejected with anger. It's unforgivable. If the return has to be made it should at least be done with tenderness, not with bitterness.'

'Something—offered with—love?' she repeated still speaking barely above a whisper. 'Ken——'

She went to him and put her arms round him from behind.

'Look at me!—please look at me.' But he shook his head and, even when she put her cheek against his arm, he only stirred sharply as though in pain.

Suddenly she knew that something infinitely precious was slipping away from her with tragic speed, and she cried, 'What shall I do? What can I say?' Then, all pride dissolving in the desperate necessity of the moment, 'I love you, Ken. I've loved you for ages; at least, it seems like that. But when you got engaged to Lucille——'

'When I *what*? Who told you that?'

'She did. I mean—she told Jeremy. She even showed him your ring——'

He said something under his breath which she thought she had misheard, for Ken was not given to picturesque swearing. Then he turned her, in a grasp that hurt, and asked hoarsely, 'Is that true, what you said?'

'Of course it's true! Why should I make up anything about Lucille?'

'No—not that! The bit about—loving me for ages.'

She nodded wordlessly, and then, in the interests of a strict truth, she said again rather forlornly, 'It *seems* like ages.'

'Oh—darling! My silly little darling!' He kissed her, almost tentatively at first and then more passionately, until she flung her arms around his neck and returned his kisses with equal passion.

'How could you be such a little idiot as to believe such nonsense about me and Lucille?'

'How could I *not* believe it?' she replied with some spirit. 'You let Lucille take the place of Enid Mountjoy on the jury.'

'I had no choice.'

'But you are—were—her agent. You said they consulted you.'

'They did—and I said she was engaged elsewhere. The ultimate in unprofessional conduct, incidentally, for which I'm ashamed. But I would do it again for you, my vengeful little love.' And smiling wryly, he stirred the pieces of torn cheque with his foot. 'I had no intention of helping her to scare you. They must have got hold of her by another channel.—What are you doing?'

For suddenly she was down on her knees, collecting the pieces of torn cheque.

'I'm putting them where they belong—in your wastepaper basket.'

'Not that piece!' He bent down and scooped up one fragment.

'What's that?' Caroline was half laughing, half anxious still.

'The bit with your signature on it, my darling, and I'm keeping it to show you belong to me.'

'But you can have my signature any time— anywhere.'

'On a contract?'

'Of course.'

'On a marriage register?'

'Of course.'

He went to the door then and called in that peremptory, slightly hectoring tone he could sometimes use, 'Dinah!'

'Yes, Mr Marshall.' Dinah came scuttling across, looking faintly anxious.

'We need you to witness—Oh, by the way, what did Lucille Duparc say in answer to my message?'

'She spoke in French, Mr Marshall, and I don't think,' Dinah added primly, 'I quite understood her.'

'Splendid.' He was already rummaging in a drawer for a contract form. 'I'm putting Caroline under contract to me for——'

'Sir Oscar said no contracts without his permission,' stated Dinah firmly. 'Not even marriage contracts.'

'He must be psychic,' said Ken. 'But it's all right—I'll deal with him. You sign here, Miss Bagshot.' And, to the great satisfaction of Dinah, he kissed the side of Caroline's cheek as she bent down to sign.

'Now you witness that, Dinah.' He pushed the form towards her, while Caroline ran her hand tenderly but somehow possessively over the back of his neck.

'I've got an agent now,' she said dreamily. 'On Saturday someone phoned to ask who my agent was and I said I had none.'

'Oh?' Ken glanced at her enquiringly. 'Who phoned to ask that?'

'I didn't know the name. He was Italian, I think.—Oh, I remember it now, though I didn't know it.' As she repeated it she seemed to be standing in the hall at home, the receiver in her hand and desolation in her heart. But that was just a bad dream. Now she was awake with the dawn of a glorious future in front of her.

'What did you say that name was?' Suddenly Ken had come to the surface, with the expression of an agent instead of a lover.

Caroline repeated it, and he reached for the telephone, exclaiming, 'Great heavens! He's the most famous of all Italian film directors!'

She watched him, smiling indulgently, and presently she sat down on the arm of his chair and put her arm round him.

'Yes, indeed,' Ken was saying. 'Certainly I represent her. As a matter of fact, she's engaged to me. No, not only professionally. Literally. Just a moment while I make sure of that.' And, putting down the receiver, he drew his signet ring from his finger and put it on Caroline's left hand.

Here's how to get this special offer from Harlequin! As simple as 1...2...3!

AUGUST
TREASURY EDITION
COUPON

1. Each month, save one Treasury Edition coupon from your favorite Romance or Presents novel.
2. In four months you'll have saved four Treasury Edition coupons (only one coupon per month allowed).
3. Then all you have to do is fill out and return the order form provided, along with the four Treasury Edition coupons required and $1.00 for postage and handling.

Mail to: Harlequin Reader Service

In the U.S.A.
P.O. Box 52040
Phoenix, AZ 85072-2040

In Canada
P.O. Box 2800, Postal Station A
5170 Yonge Street
Willowdale, Ont. M2N 6J3

Please send me my FREE copy of the Janet Dailey Treasury Edition. I have enclosed the four Treasury Edition coupons required and $1.00 for postage and handling along with this order form.

(Please Print)

NAME_____

ADDRESS_____

CITY_____

STATE/PROV._____ ZIP/POSTAL CODE_____

SIGNATURE_____
This offer is limited to one order per household.

RT1-A-2

SUPPLIES LIMITED

This special Janet Dailey offer expires January 1986.